# bff

### a girlfriend book
### u write 2gether

Other books by Lauren Myracle

*Bliss*
*Rhymes with Witches*
*ttyl*
*ttfn*
*l8r, g8r*
*Eleven*
*Twelve*
*Thirteen*
*Peace, Love, and Baby Ducks*
*Luv Ya Bunches*
*Let It Snow: Three Holiday Romances*
    (with John Green and Maureen Johnson)
*How to Be Bad* (with E. Lockhart and Sarah Mylnowski)

# bff

a girlfriend book
u write 2gether

lauren myracle

Amulet Books
New York

The Library of Congress has cataloged this book under the following control number: 2009925680

ISBN 978-0-8109-8431-8

The quiz on pages 9–17 courtesy of the Great and Fabulous Melanie Dearman.
Special thanks to Susan Homer and Elizabeth Smith for helping make this baby happen!

Text copyright © 2009 Lauren Myracle
Book design by Melissa Arnst and Interrobang Design Studio
Emoticon illustrations by Celina Carvalho

Printed and bound in U.S.A.
10 9 8 7 6 5 4 3 2 1

Amulet Books are available at special discounts when purchased in quantity for premiums and promotions as well as fundraising or educational use. Special editions can also be created to specification. For details, contact specialmarkets@abramsbooks.com or the address below.

ABRAMS
THE ART OF BOOKS SINCE 1949
115 West 18th Street
New York, NY 10011
www.abramsbooks.com

This journal was completed by us, true-blue 4-evah bff's:

melody

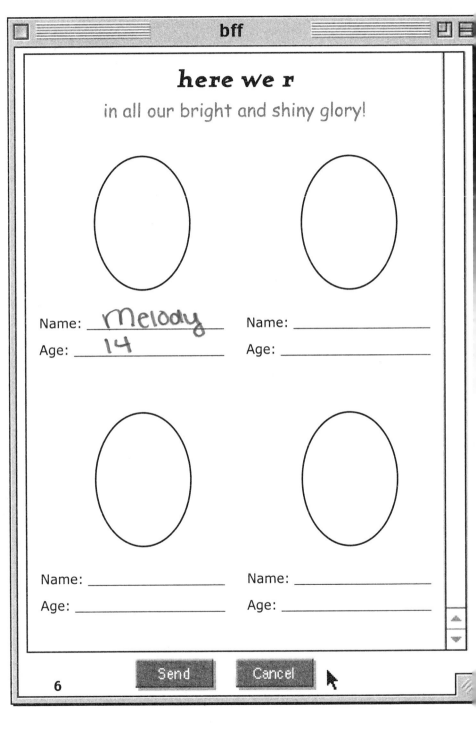

# here we r

in all our bright and shiny glory!

Name: _Melody_

Age: _14_

Name: _____

Age: _____

Name: _____

Age: _____

Name: _____

Age: _____

Send    Cancel

6

# introduction

Lauren:    Chickie-doodles! Love muffins of my heart! Hellooooooooo! I would like for you to imagine, please, that I am reaching across the space-time continuum, clasping your hands (in a completely non-pervy way), and staring deeply into your eyes (again, not pervily). Ya with me? And here is what I am saying to you, dear readers and soon-to-be-writers*:

Someone who makes you feel bad about yourself? NOT A FRIEND.

Someone who backstabs, lies, or spreads rumors about you? NOT A FRIEND.

Someone who is there for you one day, and then drops you like a hot wad of really gross . . . hot stuff the next day? NOT A FRIEND.

Someone who chooses "hot stuff" (of the non-waddy-gross sort) over you? Again: NOT. A. FRIEND.

But. Someone who loves you and makes you laugh and sees you as the radiant, perfect work in progress that you are? THAT, MY DEARIES, IS A FRIEND.

Your mission now, should you choose to accept it, is to go and honor those darling friends—and to have so much fun in the process that the world turns an even sunnier shade of gorgeous. Love breeds love

---

\* Yes, I happen to have multiple sets of arms and eyes, you literal-minded picky people! So I can hold hands with all of you and gaze into the eyes of all of you, never you fear. We can be one big hand-holding, eye-gazing fam!

breeds love, right? And one day—I'm telling ya—you will be so glad you took the time to put y'all's lists and memories and thoughts and sillinesses down on paper. Why? Because then, on those gray days we all have, you can pull this out, open it up, and find yourself once again surrounded by BFF LOVE. ♡
So what are you waiting for? GET TO IT, YOU GOOFY, LUVERLY GIRLS (AND SUPER-COOL GUYS)!!!!!

SnowAngel: scooch, lady. u've said yr piece, let us say ours! *smiles winningly to show she means no disrespect, then plops Lauren onto hospital gurney and gives a mighty shove*

zoegirl: omg. angela, i can't believe u just did that.

SnowAngel: oh, she'll be fine. she had her turn. don't u 2 want to add yr own words of encouragement?

**mad maddie: word, dude. of encouragement.**

SnowAngel: u besties out there, u bff's who're reading this. bff's make the world go 'round, y'all know that, right?

**mad maddie: true dat. i wld have died 3000 times w/o y'all.**

SnowAngel: my little sis, chrissy? i think she's sometimes jealous of the 3 of us—me, zo, and madikins—cuz she wants to have a friendship as tight as ours. and u know what i tell her? she can.

zoegirl: she *totally* can.

SnowAngel: it just takes work. work and commitment and silliness and LOVE.

**mad maddie: but y'all can do that. so off with ya, varmints!**

SnowAngel: BE TRUE! BE COOL! FILL THE WORLD WITH LOVE . . . STARTING WITH YR BUDS!!!!!! ♡

Send      Cancel

8

# quiz
## are you an Angela, a Maddie, or a Zoe?

SnowAngel:   so . . . let's get started. take this quiz with yr bff's and find out which of the winsome threesome u r most like! (and Miss I'll-Just-Read-Over-Her-Shoulder? i'm talking to u, too! and u and u! u must ALL take this quiz. i command u!)

SnowAngel:   *fluffs hair and preens in gold-plated mirror* and dahlings, do try to be me, won't u?

**mad maddie:   ur telling 'em to cheat? dude.**

SnowAngel:   um, nooooo. if they cheated, that wld make them like U. (tee-hee. KIDDING!)

zoegirl:   ignore the buffoons IMing behind the curtain. sheesh. just take the quiz. only first, predict who u think u'll each end up being . . .

1. ur at a party with people u kinda know, but not all that well. what's yr strategy, toots?

   a. i'm chatting it up with Mr. Dude, who is *so* frickin' cute that he can even get away with wearing loafers without socks. since when has flirting been a crime? ☺

   b. hrm. i'm not moping around with puppy-dog eyes, that's for sure. i'm possibly wearing some random person's cowboy hat and probably making a fool of myself. but hey, i'm having fun.

   c. i hate those kinds of parties. i'm probably sitting stiffly on the far edge of a sofa and wishing i had a book. ☹

2. wha'cha gonna do with yr life, eh?
   a. go to a good college, prolly an Ivy, and major in something like international relationships. Or English. And then join the Peace Corps for a few years . . . unless i wimp out.
   b. uh . . . go on *Survivor.* screw that—*win Survivor*!
   c. stay close to home and my friends, but *definitely* take risks and not, like, end up some boring PTA mom. oh, and whatever i do? i'll do it with style.

3. yr friends describe you as . . .
   a. practically perfect in every way.
   b. maybe a little bit shy around other people, but with unexpected bursts of boldness *if* the situation demands it.
   c. my friends describe me as "maddie." (what? they do!)

4. u see a cute guy in the hall. u know—that guy. Mr. Dude. Hottie-Pants. Monsieur Mustachio, if ur into mustaches. anyway, u've been crushing on him forever, and THERE HE IS. so whaddaya do, u luv-crazed fool?
   a. lower my voice and channel Mae West, saying sultrily, "hey, big boy. why don't you come up and see me some time?"
   b. compliment him on his shirt . . . or his hair . . . or his eyes. ooh, wait! compliment him on his shirt AND his hair AND his eyes!

Send    Cancel

c. meet his eyes—*maybe*. but then i'd prolly duck my head and scurry away. *ag.* ☺

5. yr favorite sport to watch on TV is . . .
   a. bowling. or anything with super-slo-mo. i love me some super-slo-mo.
   b. i'd rather read a book, thx. not to be rude . . .
   c. Olympic ice-skating!!! so prettiful!

6. u and yr buds have decided to get involved with the school play. u decide to . . .
   a. try out for the lead, dahlink!
   b. tell said buds that, actually, i was wrong and won't be getting involved with the school play after all. i will happily accept a bag of chips, however, if anyone wants to give me some.
   c. help out with costumes or makeup, or maybe even help direct.

7. if you were a pattern, which wld you be?
   a. polkie-dottie and pink pink pink, with one teensy tangerine-colored polka dot.
   b. gosh, prolly just . . . can I just go with white? but not a boring white. more like a nice, clean white t-shirt white.
   c. leopard print, baby!

8. u and yr lady friends r having a movie night— and it's yr turn to pick the flick! what's it gonna be?
   a. *Breakfast at Tiffany's*.

11

b. something fun WITH NO SCARINESS OR DEPRESSION, like *13 Going on 30*.

c. something extremely scary with subtle undertones of depression. um . . . i dunno. *The Ring*. or the one about the haunting in Connecticut called—oh yeah. *The Haunting in Connecticut.*

9. u've been dating a guy for three months, and u think ur both really into it. then, out of the blue, he dumps u. how do u deal?

a. i might *possibly* cry, but ONLY in private. in public i'd say the breakup was mutual. or—no, this is better—i'd go back in time using my handy-dandy time machine and dump him first, the bastard. ᴎᴇᴎᴇ lol

b. cry and cry and CRY—and, oh god, my eyes r getting puffy just thinking about it. cld we change the subject, plz?

c. well, i'd try to concentrate on other things, i guess. like schoolwork, and my friends, and i'd remind myself (or try to remind myself) that u can't force things like this. if he felt the need to break up with me, then i'm better off without him. ☺

10. a mean girl (think—cough, cough—jana) is picking on one of yr buds. ur most likely to . . .

a. make a fake announcement to the entire school about how she needs to come to the office and claim her teddy bear, since stuffed

Send    Cancel

animals r supposed to be left at home. and laugh evilly, of course.

b. hang back, see if things get better—and if they don't, i'd do whatever it takes to defend my friend.

c. do something unexpected and brilliant—like delivering baby chicks to her house!

11. what is yr biggest fear?
    a. losing the ones i love and ending up alone.
    b. not being authentic. not living a purposeful life.
    c. my *biggest* fear? um, the Stay-Puft Marshmallow Man.

12. if u were a type of chip—like, the chips u eat—u wld be . . .
    a. Doritos—crunchy, loud, and full of cheesy goodness.
    b. Pringles—yummy and neatly stacked.
    c. Bugles—quirky and fun, and hey, i can toot my own horn!

13. when it comes to school, u . . .
    a. try my best. my parents expect it of me, and i expect it of myself.
    b. go to school. and then when it comes to going *home* from school, i go home from school. and say "yay."
    c. love it! love seeing my friends. *Lurve* my friends. *LURVE!!!*

14. ur walking to the bathroom when u see the girl who's dating yr ex-boyfriend. let's call her tonnie. she's crying, so u say, "tonnie . . . what's wrong?" turns out she and yr ex have BROKEN UP, so u . . .
    a. give her a big hug and talk about how awful he is. (and maybe check in on him later, just to, ya know, see how he's doing . . .)
    b. sit next to her and listen and try to be a good person.
    c. say "the bastard!" a lot and shake my fist.

15. if yr life was a movie, u wld be played by . . .
    a. that adorable actress from *Shopaholic* whom everyone thinks is Amy Adams, but who is really Isla Fisher. or Amber Fisher, who plays Casey's bff, Ashleigh, on *Greek*, but who is unrelated to Isla Fisher.
    b. that cool but kinda jaded girl who played Juno in, erm, *Juno*.
    c. Vanessa Hudgens, but with no nudie pictures and no possibility of nudie pictures, forever and ever, amen!

16. ur about to embark on an important social outing—a date with the boy of yr dreams! what r u wearing?
    a. i'll call my bff's for advice. well, i'll call *one* of my bff's for advice, the one who understands fashion. i can't decide something like that alone!

Send     Cancel

14

b. attire: pale pink cami, fab-fitting jeans, and black open-toe heels. makeup: curled eyelashes, Big Lash mascara, this awesome new lipstick i discovered that's just the right shade of red. scent: Very Irresistible by Givenchy. 😎

c. well, first, it's highly unlikely that i'm "embarking on an important social outing." but regardless, the guy's going out with *me,* not my wardrobe.

17. a weakness of yrs is . . .
   a. please. next question?
   b. i guess . . . fear of failure? that i'm so concerned with being perfect that maybe i get too stressed-out sometimes?
   c. the way i fall for someone almost immediately, in a crush-of-the-moment sort of way.

18. yr bff's r important to u cuz . . .
   a. cuz they encourage me to try new things. cuz they accept my flaws.
   b. cuz they're my bff's!!!!! they help me keep my feet planted firmly on the ground, even when my head is floating in the clouds. and when i come crashing back down to earth, they're there to pick up the pieces.
   c. cuz they make me laugh. cuz they keep me from being *too* wild. and just say i do kinda make a huge fool of myself? they love me anyway.

# quiz results!

1: a = A, b = M, c = Z; 2: a = Z, b = M, c = A;
3: a = A, b = Z, c = M; 4: a = M, b = A, c = Z;
5: a = M, b = Z, c = A; 6: a = A, b = M, c = Z;
7: a = A, b = Z, c = M; 8: a = Z, b = A, c = M;
9: a = M, b = A, c = Z; 10: a = M, b = Z, c = A;
11: a = A, b = Z, c = M; 12: a = M, b = Z, c = A;
13: a = Z, b = M, c = A; 14: a = A, b = Z, c = M;
15: a = A, b = M, c = Z; 16: a = Z, b = A, c = M;
17: a = M, b = Z, c = A; 18: a = Z, b = A, c = M;

Name: _Melody_     Name: _____

Z's: _6_ M's: _7_ A's: _5_   Z's: ____ M's: ____ A's: ____

Name: _____   Name: _____

Z's: ____ M's: ____ A's: ____   Z's: ____ M's: ____ A's: ____

if u chose mostly Z's:

ur a ZOE! ur the girl next door: kindhearted, reserved,
and a little bit shy. u love to be around yr bff's, but new
situations and people tend to make u nervous. sometimes
this is a good thing because u think things through instead
of jumping into everything life throws yr way. but try to be
a little more open to life's opportunities, because u might
miss something great. the good thing about u is that when
u do decide to go through with something, u really commit
to it. yr relationships and experiences mean a lot to u, and

Send    Cancel

ur determined and hardworking in every aspect of yr life. ur also the best kind of bff to have. ur a bff someone can truly count on and trust. 😁

if u chose mostly M's:

ur a **MADDIE**! Tough, bold, and fun-loving, ur the wild child of the group. yr bff's always know that ur the one to go to with a nutty scheme, because few r as brave, as loyal, or as likely to carry it out as u r. 😎 ur always up for a good time, but be careful not to go too crazy. Sometimes u don't think before you act, and u end up in situations that could—and should—have been avoided. The good news is that ur resilient enough to overcome the bad stuff and, no matter what, u've got a loyal group of bff's behind u all the way.

if u chose mostly A's:

ur an *ANGELA*! ur a social butterfly. u love nothing more than being with yr bff's, celebrating the times u share with them, and making them appreciate every moment ur together. ur an optimist, too, and someone who is constantly making those around u see the brighter side of life. yr enthusiasm and spirit r appreciated by all who know u (those who matter, anyway), and yr bff's know that they can count on u no matter what. u also spend a fair amount of time hanging with the guys. 😊 when u meet a guy, you tend to immediately over-glorify him and flirt—A LOT. just be careful. if u keep playing with fire, ur bound to get burned before long. but, hey, that's why u have yr bff's. what would u do without them?

Send   Cancel

17

# what makes u & yr buds true-blue 4-evah friends, hrrmm?

| | |
|---|---|
| zoegirl: | what do u think makes yr bff yr bff? |
| SnowAngel: | as opposed to yr non-bff? |
| zoegirl: | as opposed to someone u like but who isn't necessarily a true-blue 4-ever friend. |
| SnowAngel: | 4-EVAH, u mean. true-blue 4-evah friend. or even fo-evah, to get that excellent "fo" sound in. so fun to say, yeah? fo-evah! |
| **mad maddie:** | **ok, but that sounds like FOE. which is NOT a bff and is in fact the opposite of a bff.** |
| zoegirl: | aw, mads! u R an English major-y girl after all! look at u go with the "fo" and "foe"! |
| SnowAngel: | GIRLS! FOCUS! |
| SnowAngel: | what makes besties besties? and i wld like u to answer in a haiku, please. or not. (c, zo? *I* can be all literary English-y, too!!!) |

18

Send    Cancel

SnowAngel:   aw, i'm all warm and fuzzy inside!

**mad maddie:   weird. i'm all warm and fuzzy outside—what's up with that?**

SnowAngel:   um, ok, gross??? u need to go SHAVE is what's up with that—or *u* will be the new pelt-woman!!!!

zoegirl:   hairy or not, we will always love u, sweet mads!!!!

Send   Cancel

19

# ☺ serious conversation time ☺
## jealousy

| | |
|---|---|
| SnowAngel: | *straightens necktie—which was put on for this very occasion—and assumes a SOLEMN, even SOMBER expression* |
| SnowAngel: | and now, peeps, it is time— |
| **mad maddie:** | **angela, do u need to pee?** |
| SnowAngel: | no, and shut up. it is time for a SERIOUS CONVERSATION. which I will call SERIOUS CONVERSATION TIME. |
| zoegirl: | cuz ur just nutty like that |
| SnowAngel: | that's right, now please be quiet. ahem. sometimes, some of us get . . . oh, how to say it . . . jalouse of people. |
| zoegirl: | i don't say it that way. do u say it that way, mads? |
| **mad maddie:** | **i don't even know what she's talking about. "jalouse"? it's not some sort of feminine hygiene product, is it?** |
| SnowAngel: | *shoots daggers at maddie, then smiles beatifically at dear BFF girlies* |
| SnowAngel: | what i'm asking, cuz i think it's important, is for y'all to write a little about who ur jealous of, and why, and how u handle it. i'm not saying i know how to make those feelings go away or anything . . . |
| zoegirl: | but sometimes just writing them down can defuse their power—and maybe teach u something about yrself. |
| **mad maddie:** | **yeah, like how u actually don't need to be jalouse—** |
| SnowAngel: | *jealous*! fine! don't make fun of me! |
| **mad maddie:** | **—of anyone, cuz ur cool just the way u r.** |

Send    Cancel

20

SnowAngel:   so write those jealous feelings down—and then
             poof! blow them into the wind like dandelion fluff!!!

Send    Cancel

21

# bff

## ₒ ? q & a ? ₒ
### ₒ all about GIRLS ₒ

**zoegirl:** u know something i hate?

*SnowAngel:* what, zoe? what do u hate? (am I doing a good job of being Tyra Banks?)

**mad maddie: huh?**

*SnowAngel:* i'm Tyra, and zoe is my talk show guest!

*SnowAngel:* *leans forward intimately* now. zoe. just what is it that u hate, girlfriend?

**zoegirl:** angela . . . how much caffeine have u had?

*SnowAngel:* in my lifetime? or today? or, um, in the last hour? ☺

**zoegirl:** y-y-y-yeah, nvm. what i hate—well, actually, what makes me really sad—is when girls get, like, all anti-girl for some reason. when they themselves R girls, u know? but cuz of our stupid culture, or cuz girls can sometimes be not as nice as they shld be, or whatever, they (meaning the anti-girl girls) make these big proclamations about "girls r shallow," "girls r bitchy," "i only have friends who r boys."

**mad maddie: not that there's anything wrong with boys.**

**zoegirl:** no, of course not

**mad maddie: i, for example, have lots of guy friends. but it doesn't have to be either/or, right?**

**zoegirl:** right! but can we talk about that? about how girls r stereotyped and whether those stereotypes r true or false?

Send    Cancel

22

# lauren myracle

SnowAngel:    'course! here goes. girls . . .

|  | true | false | debatable |
|---|:---:|:---:|:---:|
| make the best bff's | ☐ | ☐ | ☒ |
| r hard to get along with | ☐ | ☐ | ☒ |
| r too emotional | ☒ | ☐ | ☐ |
| can talk about their feelings | ☒ | ☐ | ☐ |
| can do lots of things at once | ☒ | ☐ | ☐ |
| r good at focusing on a goal | ☒ | ☐ | ☐ |
| r silly | ☐ | ☐ | ☒ |
| r smart | ☐ | ☐ | ☒ |
| r manipulative | ☐ | ☐ | ☒ |
| r responsible | ☒ | ☐ | ☐ |
| can't handle peer pressure | ☐ | ☐ | ☒ |
| don't stand up for themselves | ☐ | ☐ | ☒ |

Send     Cancel

|                    |       |       |       |
| ------------------ | ----- | ----- | ----- |
| _____  | ☐     | ☐     | ☐     |
| _____  | ☐     | ☐     | ☐     |

SnowAngel:   um, what r those blank lines for?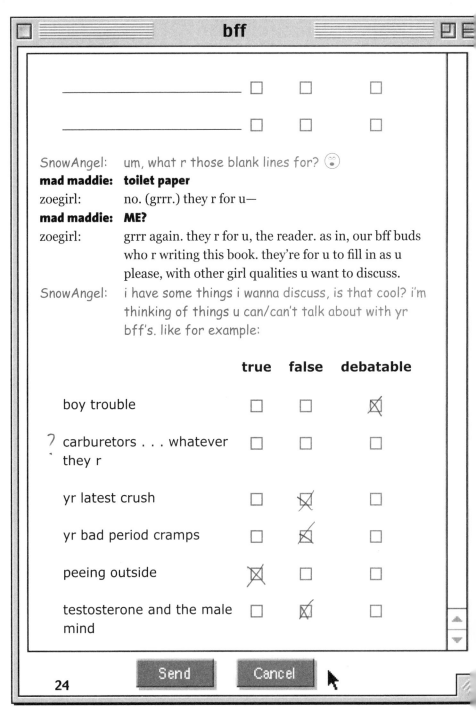
**mad maddie:   toilet paper**
zoegirl:   no. (grrr.) they r for u—
**mad maddie:   ME?**
zoegirl:   grrr again. they r for u, the reader. as in, our bff buds who r writing this book. they're for u to fill in as u please, with other girl qualities u want to discuss.
SnowAngel:   i have some things i wanna discuss, is that cool? i'm thinking of things u can/can't talk about with yr bff's. like for example:

|                              | **true** | **false** | **debatable** |
| ---------------------------- | -------- | --------- | ------------- |
| boy trouble                  | ☐        | ☐         | ☒             |
| ? carburetors . . . whatever they r | ☐        | ☐         | ☐             |
| yr latest crush              | ☐        | ☒         | ☐             |
| yr bad period cramps         | ☐        | ☒         | ☐             |
| peeing outside               | ☒        | ☐         | ☐             |
| testosterone and the male mind | ☐      | ☒         | ☐             |

Send   Cancel

24

yr fear of bunnies ☐ ☒ ☐

the fact that u think yr teacher made a pass at u ☐ ☐ ☐

whether u shld try the joint being passed around ☐ ☐ ☐

that ur secretly gay and want to come out ☐ ☐ ☐

Starbucks drinks: the relative pros and cons ☐ ☐ ☐

birth control (when u think ur ready to get it) ☐ ☐ ☐

how to save the world ☐ ☐ ☐

_____ ☐ ☐ ☐

_____ ☐ ☐ ☐

### more q&a

zoegirl: ok, now let's get specific. in terms of friends in general, i have many ppl I "strongly like," but only 2 true bff's.
SnowAngel: how about y'all?

**mad maddie:** ooo, look, she said in a deadpan voice. more of those lines. toilet paper, anyone?

_____

_____

_____

_____

_____

**mad maddie:** zo, know how u said u hate it when girls say they're only friends with guys? well, I hate it when girls say they CAN'T be friends with guys . . . the implication being that, like, hormones will get in the way or sumpin'.

zoegirl: hmm. but is there truth to it?

zoegirl: bff's! do u have more female friends or male friends? and if ur one of those girls who gets along better with guys, why?

_____

_____

_____

_____

_____

**mad maddie:** here's one: what's the most craptastic thing another girl's ever done to u?

SnowAngel: mads, u ok? did someone do something to make u mad?

**mad maddie:** **no, I just enjoy hearing stories of craptastic behavior. so spill:**

_____

_____

_____

_____

_____

**mad maddie:** **uh-huh. i see. just to show how evenhanded i am, what's the sweetest thing another girl has ever done for u?**

_____

_____

_____

_____

zoegirl: do u think girls who don't have tight female friendships r missing out?

_____

_____

_____

_____

Send     Cancel

SnowAngel:  do u get jealous of yr girlfriends? what might make u jealous?

**mad maddie:  for reals, the only thing i'm *jalouse* of is yr pink and green john deere shirt.**

_____

_____

_____

_____

**mad maddie:  do u compete with other girls over guys? what wld make u try to win the gold?**

SnowAngel:  "win the gold"? barf.

zoegirl:  she's using a sports metaphor cuz she's talking about competition.

SnowAngel:  ohhhhhh. *puts hand to side of mouth so maddie can't see and says it again: barf*

_____

_____

_____

_____

zoegirl:  if u could give girls who r younger than u one piece of advice, what wld it be?

_____

_____

Send    Cancel

**mad maddie:**   if u could give yr bff's one piece of advice, what wld it be?

SnowAngel:   ooo, ooo!!!! i've got a question to add! and it's DEEP.
SnowAngel:   if u cld give *U* one piece of advice, what wld it be?!

**mad maddie:**   alrighty then, glad we had this little talk. pip-pip, cheerio, and all that!

Send        Cancel

# ✦ ○ ✿ ☆ ○ u and yr panis ☆ ○ ✿ ☆ ○

SnowAngel:   hello, lovies. it's time to celebrate Our Womanhood!

**mad maddie:   our womanhood? urg, i just threw up in my mouth. thx for that, a.**

SnowAngel:   *smiles sweetly*

SnowAngel:   now. i have made a list of options. option 1: we form a drum circle—i myself volunteer to play the didgeridoo—and do a chant-and-response with powerful affirmations, like "release my grief!" and "fill my soul!" and "hay-o, hay-o, haaaaay-o!"

**mad maddie:   NO**

SnowAngel:   fine. option 2: we cld howl at the moon . . .

zoegirl:   no!

SnowAngel:   ok, great! option 3 it is! (i was secretly hoping u'd pick this one!!!)

**mad maddie:   oh crap**

SnowAngel:   we will now celebrate our femininity by taking a few moments to honor our squishy parts. in particular . . . the panis.

**mad maddie:   our "squishy parts"?**

zoegirl:   i don't know what she's talking about, mads. do u?

**mad maddie:   no clue.**

**mad maddie:   angela? zo and i know not of this "panis" u speak of. it's not, like, the girl version of a penis, is it?**

SnowAngel:   hardly!!!! *whistles sharply for Google*

SnowAngel:   *coos* good boy, Google! yes sir! who's my good boy?!

SnowAngel:   a panis, and i quote, is "the fat that hangs over the waist line like a separate entity." like, well, a muffin top. 🧁

30

| | |
|---|---|
| zoegirl: | omg. do i have a panis? |
| **mad maddie:** | **i do! i totally do. i am poking it right now. "hello, lurverly panis! will u be my friend?"** |
| SnowAngel: | of course yr panis will be yr friend, mads! that is THE POINT! we r girls, and girls R squishy (sometimes), and we shld embrace it. our squishiness. |
| SnowAngel: | and zo, u have a skinny-girl panis, just the teensiest little cutie-pie bulge. |
| **mad maddie:** | **a skanis** |
| SnowAngel: | yes! a skanis! and i have . . . well, a great and burning need to start going to pilates, only c'mon, that's not very likely. |
| **mad maddie:** | **u have an adorable panis, a.** |
| SnowAngel: | *makes panis talk, with belly button as mouth* why thank u, maddie! |
| **mad maddie:** | **don't thank me. thank my panis.** |
| SnowAngel: | why thank u, maddie's panis! |
| zoegirl: | i'm sorry . . . how is this empowering? |
| SnowAngel: | ah, yes. well, i have made up a delightful little game we can all play, k? it's called "with my panis," and here is how it works. i will give an inspirational quote, and u guys—and yes, bff's, ur required to join in—will complete the quote by saying . . . |
| **mad maddie:** | **WITH MY PANIS. got it!** |
| SnowAngel: | there will be a MULTITUDE of panis moments scattered like rose petals through the book; this is just the first. oh, and the person who said this first quote is Brigitte Bardot. |
| SnowAngel: | *clears throat* |
| SnowAngel: | "It is sad to grow old, but nice to ripen . . ." |
| **mad maddie:** | **WITH MY PANIS!!!!! hahahahaha!** |

| | |
|---|---|
| zoegirl: | y'all r so weird . . . |
| SnowAngel: | and now it's activity time! yaaaaaaay! |
| SnowAngel: | pretend ur back in kindergarten. ur sitting in a bitsy chair at a bitsy table, and in front of u is a big ol' honking Tupperware box filled to the brim with crayons. pretend u have a massively awesome kindergarten teacher named . . . Miss Peppermint, and she says, "All right, children. Today we will be drawing our panises. Say it with me: panises. Have fun! Be creative! And, most important of all, do NOT stay within the lines!!!" |

Send    Cancel

# ☺ serious conversation time ☺

## pressure

SnowAngel: *slips into floral dress, apron, and tightly curled grandmother wig. spritzes "eau de cookie" throughout air and pats sofa cushion invitingly*

SnowAngel: now, sugar-boogers. have u ever been pressured by a friend to do something u didn't want to do? tell grammy angela all about it . . .

_____

_____

_____

_____

_____

_____

_____

_____

_____

_____

_____

_____

_____

_____

| Send | Cancel |

# quiz
## what pattern r u?

**mad maddie:** **what if i take this quiz and find out i'm some really lame pattern? will u put me out to pasture?**

zoegirl: maddie! as if!

1. u have some money burning a hole in yr pocket. time to buy shoes! (what else is worth a girl's hard-earned cash?) what do u buy?
   - a. black stilettos (hot!)
   - b. brown ballet flats
   - c. purple clogs
   - d. pink espadrilles

2. u and yr bff's r planning a party for another friend to celebrate her new single status (go grrl power!). ur on snacks. what do u bring?
   - a. brie and crackers
   - b. sushi
   - c. hummus and pita
   - d. chocolate chip cookies

3. spring break! whoot-whoot! what's on yr to-do list for the week?
   - a. getting a tattoo
   - b. a camping trip
   - c. sewing a skirt
   - d. a tennis round-robin

Send    Cancel

34

4. yr favorite aunt offers to spring for a manicure!
   what color nail polish do u choose?
   a. a manicure? thanks, but no thanks. that's SO
      not me.
   b. Clear Ice
   c. Pure Peony
   d. Revolution Red

5. ur redecorating yr room. what's yr new look going
   to be?
   a. Cape Cod
   b. white picket fence
   c. jungle love
   d. Bohemian rhapsody

6. YAHOOTIE! it's Saturday night and the rents r out.
   what's up for u and yr bff's?
   a. Scrabble
   b. par-tay!
   c. a séance
   d. decorating cupcakes

7. it's Valentine's Day and *squeal, jump up and
   down, throw arms around yr boyfriend* yr
   boyfriend has given u the purr-fect gift. what is it?
   a. a vintage Grateful Dead tee
   b. a dozen roses
   c. fishnet stockings
   d. a poem he wrote for u

Send    Cancel

8. yr bff's would describe u as:
   a. an American classic
   b. sugar and spice
   c. the girl next door
   d. a tree hugger

9. u've been reincarnated as a flower. what kind r u?
   a. an orchid
   b. a rose
   c. a poppy
   d. a daisy

10. yr friends say ur most like this famous literary heroine:
    a. Jo March
    b. Elizabeth Bennet
    c. Nancy Drew
    d. Sara Crewe

Send    Cancel

# *quiz results!*

1: a = (L), b = S, c = T, d = F; 2: a = S, b = L, c = T, d = (F)
3: a = L, b = T, c = F, d = (S); 4: a = T, b = S, c = F, d = (L)
5: a = S, b = F, c = L, d = (T); 6: a = S, b = (L), c = T, d = F;
7: a = T, b = (S), c = L, d = F; 8: a = S, b = L, c = F, d = T;
9: a = (L), b = F, c = S, d = T; 10: a = T, b = (L), c = S, d = (F)

Name: _Melody_____    Name: _____
L's: 5  S's: 2  T's: 1  F's: 2    L's: ___ S's: ___ T's: ___ F's: ___

Name: _____    Name: _____
L's: ___ S's: ___ T's: ___ F's: ___    L's: ___ S's: ___ T's: ___ F's: ___

if u chose mostly L's: ur LEOPARD PRINT—rebellious, independent, and unique

if u chose mostly S's: ur STRIPES—refined, classic, and traditional

if u chose mostly T's: ur TIE-DYE—unpredictable, fun, and natural

if u chose mostly F'S: ur FLORAL—modest, sweet, and a little old-fashioned

Send    Cancel

# yr opinion
## socks

| | |
|---|---|
| zoegirl: | has anyone given u socks 4 a present? like yr step-grandmother, say? |
| zoegirl: | my step-grandmother gave me socks for christmas one year. she gave her un-step-grandkids thousand-dollar bonds. but me? socks. |
| **mad maddie:** | **lame!** |
| SnowAngel: | but i bet u said thank u nicely and even sent a handwritten thank-u note. |
| zoegirl: | only cuz i had to |
| zoegirl: | the socks can't be blamed for my step-grandmother's bad behavior, tho. so forget i even brought that up. that was just me being bitter. |
| SnowAngel: | is yr step-grandmother gonna read this, zo? is there the slightest teeniest chance? |
| **mad maddie:** | **HA. wld serve her right.** |
| zoegirl: | moving on. ladies, what do we think about socks and other leg/foot attire? |

**yes**   **no**

musical socks

under what circumstances OK/not OK?

_____

_____

Send    Cancel

38

'50s-style bobby socks 👍 👎

under what circumstances OK/not OK?

_____

_____

mismatched socks 👍 👎

under what circumstances OK/not OK?

tired / missing

_____

thigh-highs 👍 👎

under what circumstances OK/not OK?

ugly

_____

cutesy theme socks 👍 👎

under what circumstances OK/not OK?

holidays

_____

fishnets 👍 👎

under what circumstances OK/not OK?

*whorey*

leg warmers

under what circumstances OK/not OK?

*oldfashioned*

five-toe socks

under what circumstances OK/not OK?

*uncomfortable*

holiday socks

under what circumstances OK/not OK?

---

**mad maddie:** **or how about commando?**

SnowAngel: bare feet in shoes? ew.

zoegirl: p-ew. besides yr shoes won't last as long.

**mad maddie: ladies, u gotta live a little!**

Send    Cancel

## yes, it is that time again.
### —da da da DUM—
## ☺ **serious conversation time** ☺
### drinking and driving

| | |
|---|---|
| zoegirl: | this one's for real, tho |
| SnowAngel: | *huffs* |
| SnowAngel: | excuse me? they r all real! |
| zoegirl: | i know, but like, this one happened to me once, and it was much harder to deal with in real life than u might think. |
| zoegirl: | what wld u do if a friend got drunk at a party, and when it was time to go, she insisted on driving? and u were supposed to get a ride home with her? and she made a stink and *refused* to simply hand over the keys?! |

Send    Cancel

# quiz
## how well do u know yr bff's?
### (take this quiz together—and find out!)

SnowAngel: know what I like about being bff's? knowing every single thing there is to know about that person. am i right, or am i right?

zoegirl: um . . . well . . .

**mad maddie: i'm gonna have to go with option 3, angela. sorry.**

SnowAngel: option 3? there is no option 3. what's option 3?!

**mad maddie: that maybe u don't know every single thing there is to know about me, mwahahaha . . .**

1. when is yr bff's birthday? (duh. better get this one right!)

   yr answer: ___Dec 8th / ~~~~ Oct.13___

   yr bff's answer: _____

   did u get it right? ___yes_____

2. where was yr bff born?

   yr answer: ___hospital?_____

   yr bff's answer: _____

   did u get it right? _____

3. what's yr bff's favorite color?

   yr answer: ___baby blue_____

Send    Cancel

yr bff's answer: _____

did u get it right? _____

4. what's yr bff's favorite song to listen to when she's down? when she's up?

yr answer: _____

yr bff's answer: _____

did u get it right? _____

5. who is yr bff's secret crush?

yr answer: ___Caleb, ? no clue___

yr bff's answer: _____

did u get it right? _____

6. who does yr bff admire most in the world?

yr answer: ___ME! duh___

yr bff's answer: _____

did u get it right? _____

7. has yr bff ever been kissed? if so, by whom?

yr answer: ___no, yes___

yr bff's answer: _____

did u get it right? _____

Send    Cancel

8. does yr bff go for whipped cream or no whipped cream on a sundae?

yr answer: _yes!._____

yr bff's answer: _____

did u get it right? _____

9. what part of yr bff's favorite movie does she watch over and over and over? (u know u do it, too!)

yr answer: _____

yr bff's answer: _____

did u get it right? _____

10. what size feet does yr bff have?

yr answer: _____

yr bff's answer: _____

did u get it right? _____

11. what is yr bff's secret phobia? (spiders? monsters under the bed? heights?)

yr answer: _____

yr bff's answer: _____

did u get it right? _____

Send    Cancel

12. is yr bff a dog person or a cat person (or some other kind of animal person)?

yr answer: _____

yr bff's answer: _____

did u get it right? _____

13. if yr bff could hop on a plane and go anywhere, where would it be?

yr answer: _____

yr bff's answer: _____

did u get it right? _____

14. does yr bff make her bed every morning?

yr answer: _____

yr bff's answer: _____

did u get it right? _____

15. what is yr bff's fantasy job? (actress? scientist? first sk8r-chick president?)

yr answer: _____

yr bff's answer: _____

did u get it right? _____

Send    Cancel

16.  what is yr bff's favorite pig-out food?

yr answer: _____

yr bff's answer: _____

did u get it right? _____

17.  yr bff's fairy godmother gives her $1000.00. what does she do with the money?

yr answer: _____

yr bff's answer: _____

did u get it right? _____

18.  yr bff's boyfriend gives her a flower, and it's her favorite. what is it?

yr answer: _____

yr bff's answer: _____

did u get it right? _____

19.  yr bff finds out her boyfriend is cheating on her. what does she do?

yr answer: _____

yr bff's answer: _____

did u get it right? _____

Send    Cancel

20. if yr bff could solve any of the world's problems, what would it be?

yr answer: _____

yr bff's answer: _____

did u get it right? _____

# quiz results!

**1–5 correct answers:** u need to spend a little more time together! but don't worry—bff's have to start somewhere!

**6–10 correct answers:** ur bff's-in-training! and now u know loads more about each other than u did.

**11–15 correct answers:** u've got a good thing going! ur on yr way to bff-stardom!

**16–20 correct answers:** ur true-blue 4-evah bff's! u cld fool an immigration official! like if u married yr bestie, but just to get her a green card, and the immigration ppl made u take a "how well do u 2 know each other" test? U WLD ACE IT, BABY!!!!

| | |
|---|---|
| **mad maddie:** | **uh . . . yay, wh-hoo, and all that. but a word to the wise: if u fell into that last category? u seriously need to add some mystery to yr life.** |
| **mad maddie:** | **and i'm not kidding. at all.** |
| **mad maddie:** | **(seriously!)** |

# 5 things about u (and u and u and u) that wld gross ppl out if they knew

**mad maddie:** i'll even start, just to show u how it's done. um, angela and zoe, wld one of y'all find a locker and hide in it, please?

SnowAngel: no

zoegirl: why?!

**mad maddie:** so u can pop out and be, like, the straight guy—gal—for my joke. please?!

zoegirl: grrr

**mad maddie:** and look! there's a locker right there! holy crap, it's like . . . magic!

zoegirl: fine, i'm—ouch—in the locker. cld we move this along?

**mad maddie:** sure. heyyy, zoe!

zoegirl: what?

**mad maddie:** no, u have to pop yr head out and say very chirpily, "yes, maddie?"

**mad maddie:** take 2. heyyy, zoe!

zoegirl: yes, maddie?

**mad maddie:** why did the girl named me leave her toenail polish on for 8 months?

zoegirl: i don't know, maddie. why did the girl named u leave her toenail polish on for 8 months?

SnowAngel: ewww.

**mad maddie:** to find out how long it takes for toenails to completely grow out! get it? get it?!

SnowAngel: *shudders*

Send    Cancel

48

SnowAngel:   now it's yr turn, so, um, go for it. if u want.
**mad maddie:   zo? u can come out of the locker now . . .**

Name: _____

1. _____

2. _____

3. _____

4. _____

5. _____


Name: _____

1. _____

2. _____

3. _____

4. _____

5. _____


Name: _____

1. _____

2. _____

3. _____

4. _____

5. _____

Send     Cancel

Name: _____

1. _____

2. _____

3. _____

4. _____

5. _____

**mad maddie:** **aw, man. u besties are a disgusting lot. way to go!!!!**

SnowAngel: um, ur praising them for being disgusting? ☺

**mad maddie:** **dudes. ppl think girls shld be delicate and sweet and proper . . . u do NOT have to listen!**

**mad maddie:** **whoa—an ant just fell out of my hair. a live ant. it landed on my keyboard, and now it's crawling away. byeas, little ant friend!**

SnowAngel: oh, maddie.

**mad maddie:** **rejoice in my gross-ness!!!!! yee-haw!!!!**

### time out for . . .
# u and yr panis

SnowAngel: this quote's from a French guy named albert camus.

SnowAngel: "Great works r often born on a street corner or in a restaurant's revolving door . . ."

**mad maddie:** **WITH MY PANIS!!!!!**

**mad maddie:** **only now it's stuck! help me, angela! my panis is stuck in the revolving door!**

Send    Cancel

50

# yr bff playlist
## happy tunes

**mad maddie:** **also known as BFF Boogy-licious Dance Tunes!**

SnowAngel: we think y'all shld create a playlist just for this book! a playlist of spazzy-happy-sunshine songs. (we'll make a playlist of mellow songs l8r.)

SnowAngel: and . . . ooo! ooo! mads, I totally like yr title, but u know what else they cld name their playlist? "SUPERFLYINGTACKLEPOUNCE!" *claps hands and bounces like a maniac*

zoegirl: here's what we want u to do. like a game of hot potato, go round and round and add songs until u've got enough spaztastic faves to dance the night away!

zoegirl: ready . . . set . . . go!

_____

_____

_____

_____

_____

_____

_____

_____

_____

_____

Send    Cancel

# yr opinion
## food combinations

zoegirl: ok, mads. JUST FOR U, i tried soy milk and raisin bran this morning.

**mad maddie: AND?**

SnowAngel: *turns green*

zoegirl: i don't c myself making a habit of it . . . but it wasn't bad, actually.

**mad maddie: ha ha HA! next u'll be wearing tie-dyed skirts like pelt-woman!**

SnowAngel: u should talk! u drank prune juice once!

**mad maddie: don't u be dissing my prune juice, lady. it is delish with seltzer.**

SnowAngel: what to the evs. *rolls eyes*

**mad maddie: yr turn, bff's. weigh in on these scrumptious combos.**

|  | yes | no |
|---|---|---|
| chocolate and peanut butter |  |  |
| popcorn and M&Ms |  |  |
| bacon and chocolate |  |  |
| french fries and mayonnaise |  |  |
| Twizzlers used as straws to suck up Coke |  |  |
| cashews (salted, of course) and mini-marshmallows |  |  |

Send      Cancel

marshmallows, period—any size, just by themselves

pimiento cheese and half a fly

duck (cooked) and orange marmalade

fingernails and those little bits of skin that come off when u bite them, which u shouldn't, because that's disgusting, u fingernail-biting fool

saltines and butter

soy milk and raisin bran

normal milk and Nestlé Quik (if u answer "no" to this one, do not pass go and do not collect $200.00. seriously.)

stale Certs from the dollar store, again just by themselves

what other bizarre-o food combos float yr boat?

_____

_____

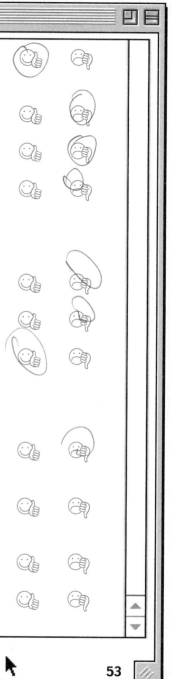

Send   Cancel

53

# yr fave books ~~EVER~~ EVAH!

**mad maddie:** **u did that, didn't u, angela?**

SnowAngel: *glances around innocently*

SnowAngel: I'm sorry . . . what?

**mad maddie:** **the strikeout**

SnowAngel: r u talking sports again, mads? u know i don't like hockey.

**mad maddie:** **no, I mean on the top of the page where u . . .**

**mad maddie:** **nvm, not worth it. zo, this one's yr baby, yeah? u wanna bring it on home?**

zoegirl: sure. when it comes to books, there r the ones yr English teacher assigns, and the ones yr parents buy u, and sometimes very occasionally they turn out to be . . . not exactly as scintillating as u might hope.

**mad maddie:** **translation for the non-zoe's of the world: BORING AS ALL GET-OUT.**

zoegirl: but then there r the books that TOUCH YR SOUL and MAKE U A BETTER PERSON and KEEP U UP ALL NIGHT, reading to the very last page.

SnowAngel: those r the books that deserve their own list. ☺

zoegirl: yeah. so pass this from bff to bff, taking turns writing down the books that top yr best-ever list. then, when u need a book to lift u up, u'll know where to go!

_____

_____

_____

_____

Send    Cancel

Send  Cancel

# something fun to do!
## *googlewhack!*

**mad maddie:** do u ever get so overwhelmed u feel like yr head is going 2 explode?

zoegirl: not in such a graphic way, no.

SnowAngel: i never get overwhelmed. *ahem* ☺

**mad maddie:** don't make me laff! anyhoo here's my distraction therapy.

**mad maddie:** go to google and type 2 words into the search area. yr goal is 2 get a "googlewhack," which in layman's terms means to get only 1 hit. for example, "crapulent porker" *used* to be a googlewhack . . . until too many peeps ruined it.

**mad maddie:** but if u try reallllly hard, i bet u can find yr very own!

zoegirl: i'm not sure what the point is.

**mad maddie:** the point is there IS no point.

SnowAngel: lol! i'll try it after my own personal distraction therapy . . . youtubing ninja cat yet again!

**mad maddie:** but make sure u use real words . . . as in words that r in the dictionary. like madigan's pantaloons (520 hits!) or etui yautia (239!). write down yr words and scores.

_____

_____

_____

_____

_____

Send     Cancel

time out for . . .
## u and yr panis

| | |
|---|---|
| **mad maddie:** | **all right, i want to come up with the quote this time—and zo, i want U to answer back.** |
| **mad maddie:** | **this one's from a writer named Erica Jong: "Everyone has talent. What is rare is the courage to follow that talent . . ."** |
| zoegirl: | with my panis. ha ha. |
| SnowAngel: | oh, zoe, u and yr panis r so brave!!!!! |

# bff

## u know u want it! that's right, sistahs, it's
# ☺ serious conversation time ☺
### cheating

| | |
|---|---|
| zoegirl: | um, u ask, angela. i don't want to ask the question. |
| SnowAngel: | why? |
| **mad maddie:** | **cuz she doesn't want ppl to call her a goody-goody and throw shoes at her.** |
| zoegirl: | that is a horrible idea to plant in ppl's heads, and if anyone throws even a single shoe at mc, i'm blaming U. |
| **mad maddie:** | **if anyone throws a single shoe at u, give them to me!** |
| SnowAngel: | what if the shoe is filled to the brim with B.O.? somebody's stinky foot B.O.?!!! 👣 |
| zoegirl: | omg, y'all get OFF TOPIC more quickly than my grandmother. |
| zoegirl: | the serious question is this: what wld u do if a friend asked u to help her cheat? or give her the answer to an exam question? |
| **mad maddie:** | **or lend her yr booty shorts?** |
| zoegirl: | no! shut up! the question is about morals and integrity, NOT booty shorts. |
| zoegirl: | just answer it, ok? |

_____

_____

_____

_____

_____

Send     Cancel

# lauren myracle

Send  Cancel

# ? ? q&a ? ?
## ?. all about guys ?

SnowAngel: *rubs hands gleefully*
SnowAngel: oh dahlinks! it ees time to talk about ze boy-eez!
**mad maddie: r u using an accent? r u going to start sprinkling "jalouse" thru yr sentences again?**
SnowAngel: maybe yes, maybe no.
SnowAngel: but vat i reelly vant to talk about ees ze delightfulness of ze opposite zex.
SnowAngel: um, sex. ☺
zoegirl: and the un-delightfulness, 2 . . .
SnowAngel: *flutters fingers dismissively* yes, yes, of course. shall ve get started?
SnowAngel: those creatures we call "males" . . .

|  | true | false | debatable |
|---|:---:|:---:|:---:|
| make the best bff's | ☐ | ☐ | ☐ |
| r hard to get along with | ☐ | ☐ | ☐ |
| r smarter than girls | ☐ | ☐ | ☐ |
| r dumber than girls | ☐ | ☐ | ☐ |
| r less mature than girls | ☐ | ☐ | ☐ |
| hate romantic movies | ☐ | ☐ | ☐ |

Send    Cancel

60

|  | true | false | debatable |
|---|:---:|:---:|:---:|
| can't talk about their feelings | ☐ | ☐ | ☐ |
| know what they want | ☐ | ☐ | ☐ |
| r manipulative | ☐ | ☐ | ☐ |
| can't handle peer pressure | ☐ | ☐ | ☐ |
| boss girls around | ☐ | ☐ | ☐ |
| _____ | ☐ | ☐ | ☐ |
| _____ | ☐ | ☐ | ☐ |

SnowAngel: ooo, so delish, despite their often obnoxiousness. let's talk about them some more!

zoegirl: u know how we checked off girl-to-girl topics of conversation? let's do the same, but girl-to-guy.

**mad maddie: like, what things u'd rather talk to a guy about? or just what things u can talk to a guy about?**

zoegirl: either. yr call.

SnowAngel: let's do it!

Send      Cancel

| | true | false | debatable |
|---|---|---|---|
| boy trouble | ☐ | ☐ | ☐ |
| mustaches, and how much self-confidence a guy must possess to rock one | ☐ | ☐ | ☐ |
| yr latest crush | ☐ | ☐ | ☐ |
| yr bad period cramps | ☐ | ☐ | ☐ |
| whether yr zit is bigger than Manhattan | ☐ | ☐ | ☐ |
| the latest frappuccino flavor | ☐ | ☐ | ☐ |
| the down-and-dirty deets of yr sex life, such as it is (and no, we don't necessarily mean "sex" itself. altho we don't un-mean it, either . . .) | ☐ | ☐ | ☐ |
| the fact that u think yr teacher made a pass at u | ☐ | ☐ | ☐ |
| whether u shld try the joint being passed around | ☐ | ☐ | ☐ |
| that ur secretly gay and want to come out | ☐ | ☐ | ☐ |

|  | true | false | debatable |
|---|:---:|:---:|:---:|
| what u want to be when u grow up | ☐ | ☐ | ☐ |
| birth control (when u think ur ready to get it) | ☐ | ☐ | ☐ |
| how to save the world | ☐ | ☐ | ☐ |
| _____ | ☐ | ☐ | ☐ |
| _____ | ☐ | ☐ | ☐ |

### more q&a

SnowAngel:  how many close guy friends do u have? have u ever
           had crushes on any of them? even a teeny little bit?

_____

_____

_____

_____

_____

zoegirl:    what's the meanest thing a guy's ever done or said to
         u? how did u handle it?

**mad maddie:  yeah—and want me to go t.p. his house for u?**

Send    Cancel

63

SnowAngel: what's the sweetest thing a guy (who isn't yr boyfriend) has ever done for u? what did u say or do in return?

**mad maddie: do u think girls who don't have guy friends r missing out?**

Send     Cancel

64

| | |
|---|---|
| zoegirl: | say ur really good friends with a guy— |
| **mad maddie:** | **ok! i'm really good friends with a guy!** |
| zoegirl: | haha |
| zoegirl: | but say ur friends with a guy, and he tells u he's crushing on a girl in yr class. wld u be jealous? |
| SnowAngel: | big crush or baby crush? |
| zoegirl: | hmm. either. both! |

_____

_____

_____

_____

| | |
|---|---|
| zoegirl: | sometimes, with guys, i feel like i have to work super hard to prove to them (or to myself?) that i'm just as smart/witty/capable as they r, or whatever. is that just me, or do y'all feel that way 2? |

_____

_____

_____

_____

| | |
|---|---|
| **mad maddie:** | **what can u learn from the guys in yr life?** |
| SnowAngel: | or what have u learned, already? |

_____

_____

Send    Cancel

**mad maddie:** ok, ANGELA (yes, i'm staring at u), there is an obvious follow-up to yr "what advice wld u give guys" question.

**mad maddie:** what advice wld u give YRSELF about guys?!

SnowAngel: *smiles and crosses legs demurely at ankles*

SnowAngel: well, ladies, i think we have accomplished quite a lot here.

zoegirl: i do, too. sometimes i think we need to remember that guys and girls r more alike than different, u know?

**mad maddie:** uh . . . not sure i agree. i mean, we're all human, sure. but there is something called "testosterone" that we just don't have.

SnowAngel: thank god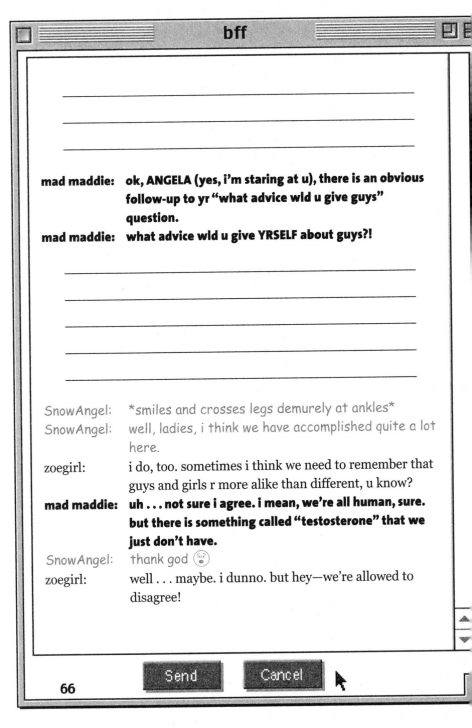

zoegirl: well . . . maybe. i dunno. but hey—we're allowed to disagree!

Send    Cancel

# ☺ **serious conversation time** ☺
## a tricky situation

**zoegirl:** ok, so when i was in 10th grade, i kinda had this . . . thing with one of my teachers.

**SnowAngel:** his name was Mr. H. and u didn't have a THING, or at least, not a thing thing.

**mad maddie:** more of an inappropriate "i'm a teacher and i'm going to hit on u, little girl" type of thing.

**zoegirl:** um. sorta.

**zoegirl:** but just for the sake of conversation . . . in the real world, ppl with huge age differences fall in love and get married all the time.

**SnowAngel:** but not when one of them is in school and the other is her teacher. zo, shld i be worried that ur, like, hedging on this all of a sudden?

**zoegirl:** no! at least not in terms of me and mr. h. i just think it's worth talking about, is all.

**mad maddie:** all right, then. let's talk.

**mad maddie:** bff-sters: what wld u do if yr teacher made a pass at u? or if some other old-head made a pass at u? or—here's a twist—what if one of yr friends (who was your age) made a pass at someone much older.

_____

_____

_____

_____

# top 10 qualities
# in a good boyfriend
### (or, if u swing the other way, girlfriend who's more than just a friend)

**mad maddie:** can i tell a cute story about ian?

SnowAngel: of course

**mad maddie:** it's from an email he sent me last nite. first i've gotta give u the context. remember last month when he decided to grow a mustache, and i told y'all privately that as far as bad ideas went, that one ranked right up there with wearing a banana hammock speedo?

SnowAngel: banana hammock speedo. tee-hee.

**mad maddie:** but last nite i was looking at ian's facebook pics, and there was one of him during the (short-lived) days of the 'stache. AND HE LOOKED SERIOUSLY DASHING, DUDES!

SnowAngel: awwww. "dashing," such an old-fashioned word.

zoegirl: and ian *always* looks dashing, mads. mustache or no mustache.

**mad maddie:** yeah yeah. so i sent a message saying he shld consider growing it back, and now i'm gonna paste in his response:

Well, Mads, I've thought about bringing back the 'stache, but it takes an unsustainable amount of self-confidence to rock one. No matter how big my mental broom, it was difficult to sweep away the suspicion that the thing growing on my upper lip wasn't simply ridiculous. It lengthened by one the list of thoughts

Send   Cancel

that keep me awake at night: Why does a girl as
great as u love a guy like me? Am I living up to my
potential? When I'm at the moment of death, will
I feel happy with everything I've done, or will I go
cravenly, regretfully? And does this mustache make
me look like a tool?

**mad maddie:** **isn't that funny and awesome and just, u know, cool?**

SnowAngel: absolutely adorkable ☺

zoegirl: wow, i kinda love that. i kinda want to print it out and
thumbtack it on my wall.

**mad maddie:** **i know, right? smarts look good on a guy, sez i.**

SnowAngel: sez me, 2. definitely on my "top ten list of boyfriend
essentials"

zoegirl: what r the others?

SnowAngel: *gives a brisk clap* let's find out! each bff gets to
check off ten.

### yr names or initials:   ____  ____  ____  ____

| | | | | |
|---|---|---|---|---|
| good-looking | ☐ | ☐ | ☐ | ☐ |
| supersmart | ☐ | ☐ | ☐ | ☐ |
| life of the party | ☐ | ☐ | ☐ | ☐ |
| talented | ☐ | ☐ | ☐ | ☐ |
| funny | ☐ | ☐ | ☐ | ☐ |
| kind | ☐ | ☐ | ☐ | ☐ |

Send    Cancel

# bff

**yr names or initials:** _____ _____ _____ _____

| | | | | |
|---|---|---|---|---|
| ambitious | ☐ | ☐ | ☐ | ☐ |
| sexy | ☐ | ☐ | ☐ | ☐ |
| strong | ☐ | ☐ | ☐ | ☐ |
| gentle | ☐ | ☐ | ☐ | ☐ |
| confident | ☐ | ☐ | ☐ | ☐ |
| athletic | ☐ | ☐ | ☐ | ☐ |
| spontaneous | ☐ | ☐ | ☐ | ☐ |
| honest | ☐ | ☐ | ☐ | ☐ |
| poetic | ☐ | ☐ | ☐ | ☐ |
| responsible | ☐ | ☐ | ☐ | ☐ |
| logical | ☐ | ☐ | ☐ | ☐ |
| charming | ☐ | ☐ | ☐ | ☐ |
| polite | ☐ | ☐ | ☐ | ☐ |
| irreverent | ☐ | ☐ | ☐ | ☐ |

Send    Cancel

**yr names or initials:** ___ ___ ___ ___

sarcastic ☐ ☐ ☐ ☐

creative ☐ ☐ ☐ ☐

a badass ☐ ☐ ☐ ☐

a teacher's pet ☐ ☐ ☐ ☐

levelheaded ☐ ☐ ☐ ☐

talkative ☐ ☐ ☐ ☐

easygoing ☐ ☐ ☐ ☐

affectionate ☐ ☐ ☐ ☐

generous ☐ ☐ ☐ ☐

hardworking ☐ ☐ ☐ ☐

direct ☐ ☐ ☐ ☐

mustachioed ☐ ☐ ☐ ☐

_____ ☐ ☐ ☐ ☐

_____ ☐ ☐ ☐ ☐

Send   Cancel

# boredom busters for babes
## a list
## (by Angela)

SnowAngel:   sweeties, it is time for some good plain FUN. it is
             time not for a serious question, but for a totally un-
             serious section i call . . . boredom busters! For babes!
             BOREDOM BUSTERS FOR BABES! ☆🎆☆🎆☆

SnowAngel:   on my count, k? three . . . two . . . one . . .

1.  on a separate piece of paper, compose an original song
    about being bff's. each person writes one line . . .
    bonus points if u rhyme!

2.  have a cheeseball race. using only yr nose, push a
    cheeseball through an obstacle course. up the stairs?
    no prob! winner eats all.

3.  see who can peel a banana with her toes the fastest
    (or at all).

4.  see who can fit the most clippies in her hair? the
    most elastics? (take pics and post them to yr favorite
    author's website!!!)

5.  make haute couture gowns from household items
    (aluminum foil, toilet paper, garbage bags, soda
    cans . . . ). all u need is a red carpet, lights, and a
    camera and ur set to host a fashion show.

Send    Cancel

6. see who can type a love letter to her crush the fastest using only her nose?

7. create a sculpture out of french fries. work together or have a modern art contest. (who says fast food has to be bad for u?)

8. speaking of art, how about an artistic pizza-eating contest? who knew u could eat something into the shape of new jersey? or a vampire bat?

9. take yr houseplants for a walk. (seriously, gals. u and yr plants need some fresh air!)

10. give yrselves beehive hairdos! don't forget to take photographs!

list yr own ideas here:

_____

_____

_____

_____

_____

_____

_____

_____

# another fun thing to do!
## yr celebrity match

SnowAngel:  who wld u set up yr bff with? don't hold back! there
r plenty of celebs who must be dying to date her,
altho it's ok to go for a fictional guy (or girl if she
prefers), too. for instance maddie + edward cullen =
crazy love. ☺

**mad maddie:  angela! not my type AT ALL! i don't need rescuing!**

_____ + _____ = true love always ♡

_____ + _____ = marriage and kids—

ten of 'em! ☺

_____ + _____ = never a dull moment

_____ + _____ = crazy love ☻

_____ + _____ = double trouble

_____ + _____ = soul mates ☺

_____ + _____ = hot and cold

_____ + _____ = Romeo and Juliet . . .

fi-yer!!!! ☺

_____ + _____ = _____

_____ + _____ = _____

_____ + _____ = _____

_____ + _____ = _____

Send     Cancel

74

# ☺ serious conversation time ☺
## boys and bff's

| | |
|---|---|
| zoegirl: | my turn to ask a serious question. |
| SnowAngel: | *waves spooky hands up and down like a fortune teller* ooooooooo! |
| zoegirl: | what wld u do if one of yr bff's—or one of yr friends in general—asked out the guy u were crushing on? and she knew u were crushing on him, and that u'd been crushing on him for like yr whole life? but to make it more complicated, let's say that nothing's ever happened between u and this guy . . . and there does seem to be the possibility of, like, vibes between him and yr friend . . . |
| zoegirl: | seriously, what do u do? |

_____

_____

_____

_____

_____

_____

_____

_____

_____

_____

Send    Cancel

# top 10 ways to tell . . .
## that yr crush likes u back!

| | |
|---|---|
| zoegirl: | so how do u know if yr crush is into u? there r signs— |
| SnowAngel: | i have a simple solution: flirt with the boy! |
| zoegirl:. | but angela, not all of us r as good at flirting as u r. |
| **mad maddie:** | **make that none of us** |
| SnowAngel: | *tilts head, smiles, and fluffs hair* |
| zoegirl: | in fact, some of us r deathly afraid of flirting, cuz what if the guy in question is totally not into us? |
| **mad maddie:** | **yeah?! and thinks we're disgusting! and writes mean things about us on the bathroom walls!** |
| zoegirl: | ok, thx, mads. thx for making my nightmare that much worse. |
| **mad maddie:** | **oh, shut yr piehole. u & doug r gonna get married, and u know it. u shldn't be flirting with other guys anywayz.** |
| zoegirl: | yes, but *hypothetically*. what if I *hypothetically* wanted to flirt with a guy, but cldn't get up the nerve due to fear of rejection made ten thousand times worse by the callous speculations of my supposed bff? |
| **mad maddie:** | **heh heh heh. and what if after Jerky Guy wrote all that mean stuff HE TAPED UP A PICTURE OF U, TOO?! and it was like from the 5th grade, and yr hair was yanked back in a super-tight pony, and u had braces, and yr mouth was smiling, but yr eyes were the panicked eyes of a girl holding in explosive diarrhea?** |
| SnowAngel: | omg. once again, y'all r making this way too complicated. |
| SnowAngel: | i've made a list of "signs that a boy likes ya." rank |

76

each one from surest (1) to least sure (10). and feel free to add yr own.

\_\_\_ He's always up for a fun IM or text convo.

\_\_\_ When he sees me in the hall, he smiles and stops to chat.

\_\_\_ He compliments me on how I look.

\_\_\_ He often hangs out by my locker.

\_\_\_ He likes to make me laugh.

\_\_\_ He shows up often at the places I like to chill with my friends.

\_\_\_ He mentions after-school activities and asks if I'm planning to attend.

\_\_\_ He shows up at my games and cheers for me.

\_\_\_ He offers me rides home from school.

\_\_\_ One of his buds asks my bff if I've got a date for the upcoming dance.

\_\_ _____

\_\_ _____

| Send | Cancel | ▲ ▼ |

~~He posts pictures in the boys' bathroom of u in the 5th grade, looking as if u've got explosive diarrhea coming on.~~

zoegirl:       no. ignore the last one, obviously. (maddie!!!!)

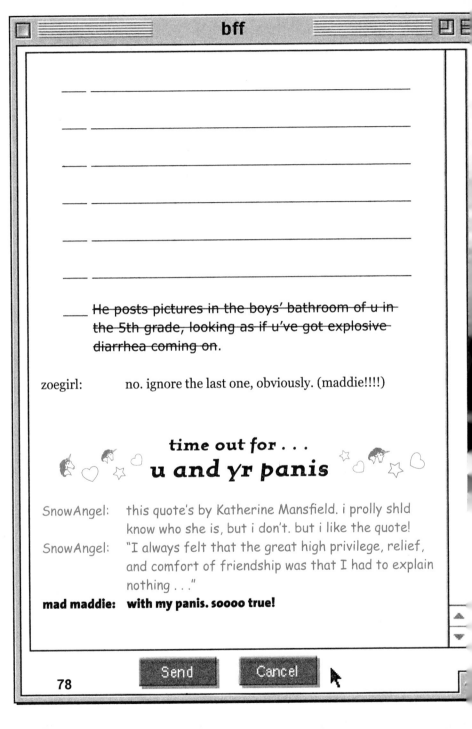

### time out for . . .
# u and yr panis

SnowAngel:  this quote's by Katherine Mansfield. i prolly shld
                know who she is, but i don't. but i like the quote!

SnowAngel:  "I always felt that the great high privilege, relief,
                and comfort of friendship was that I had to explain
                nothing . . ."

**mad maddie:  with my panis. soooo true!**

🗗 ▤

# another fun thing to do!
## imagine yr fantasy first date

SnowAngel:   juiciness time. describe yr fantasty first date,
               starting with . . . who's the lucky guy for each bff?!

Name of guy: _____     Name of guy: _____

Name of guy: _____     Name of guy: _____

zoegirl:      okay, nice. and where r y'all gonna go? (this can say A
            LOT about the 2 of y'all as a couple, so think carefully!)

____ bowling

____ out for coffee

____ video gaming at his house

____ candlelit dinner

____ a movie

____ a school dance

____ a sporting event

____ the beach

____ a party

____ a museum

____ to hear a band

. . . or?

____ _____

    Send     Cancel

___ _____

**mad maddie:   how the heck r u getting there?**

___ my car—I like to keep my freedom

___ his car, and it's a bitchin' _____

___ a horse and carriage

___ bikes

___ a boat

___ a Vespa

___ a private jet (duh!)

. . . or?

___ _____

___ _____

**mad maddie:   what songs ya gonna listen to?**

_____

_____

_____

_____

SnowAngel:   crazy question
SnowAngel:   how many people will go? i mean, the 2 of u might be
             perfect but. . .

| Send | Cancel |

zoegirl: i know where ur going with this. it might be easier to get to know him with other ppl around?

_____

_____

_____

_____

zoegirl: does he foot the bill?

_____

SnowAngel: so what r u gonna wear?!!! every. single. detail. please!!!!

attire: _____

_____

_____

_____

scent: _____

_____

_____

_____

**mad maddie: what's HE gonna wear? long as u don't say "a banana hammock speedo," we're ok ...**

Send    Cancel

attire: _____

_____

_____

_____

scent: _____

_____

_____

_____

zoegirl: any other details u want to add? like, the amazing meal, the quirky indie movie, the unexpectedly sweet remarks he makes?

zoegirl: dream it, say it, make it happen!

_____

_____

_____

_____

SnowAngel: at what point will u know HE IS THE ONE?

___ when ur talking about _____.

___ when he looks at u with his sexy, soulful eyes and

says "_____."

___ when he holds yr hand while u r _____.

Send    Cancel

\_\_\_ when u find yrself saying "_____."

\_\_\_ when u feel all_____.

. . . or?

\_\_\_ _____

\_\_\_ _____

\_\_\_ _____

**mad maddie:  let's talk smooching! do u get a good-night kiss?** 😊

\_\_\_ not on a first date

\_\_\_ he kisses my hand—like a perfect gentleman (the

sexy kind!!!)

\_\_\_ just one peck—on the cheek

\_\_\_ definitely. we've been liplocked all night!

zoegirl:        then he says, "so when do i get to c u again?"

SnowAngel:   awwww! be still, my heart! ♡

Send    Cancel

83

# ☺ serious conversation time ☺
## bff's and boys

SnowAngel: ok. once upon a time there were 2 lovely friends, and one of them liked this guy, but the other one kinda did too, and—

zoegirl: no, no, no. if yr talking about doug . . .

**mad maddie: oh, she's talking about doug.**

zoegirl: then STOP RIGHT THERE.

zoegirl: u didn't like doug. u just liked doug liking u.

SnowAngel: noooo. i didn't like doug liking me. i just didn't like doug not liking me all of a sudden and choosing to like u instead, when u didn't even like him yourself!

zoegirl: except i did. i was just afraid to tell u.

**mad maddie: good lord, ppl. ANCIENT HISTORY.**

**mad maddie: here's a thought. forget doug, since that all worked out anyway.**

SnowAngel: *sniffs* eventually

**mad maddie: what's worth talking about is this: what wld u do if someone's boyfriend—**

SnowAngel: someone's *legitimate* bf, not a fantasy bf

zoegirl: irrelevant! doug became my legitimate bf!!!!!

**mad maddie: forget doug!**

**mad maddie: bff's: what wld u do if a friend's bf made a pass at u?**

_____

_____

_____

_____

Send     Cancel

# yr bff playlist
## attractivate

SnowAngel: sexy sirens sing sexy songs!

**mad maddie: or they listen to 'em, anywayz**

zoegirl: that's right, it's romantic playlist time. write down the name of one sexy song, then pass the list to yr bff's. go round and round until u have a killer playlist of old and new tunes that will slay yr guy—and make him swear undying love for u.

_____

_____

_____

_____

_____

_____

_____

_____

_____

_____

_____

_____

_____

Send    Cancel

# yr opinion
## guys and fashion

SnowAngel: let's do the thumb's up/thumb's down thing for guys and their fashion choices. and let's start with doug.

zoegirl: omg, here we go again.

**mad maddie: oh, but I'm with her this time, zo. does doug wear boxers? briefs? banana hammock?**

zoegirl: no, yick, and none of yr beeswax, u sickos!

SnowAngel: hee hee 😁

SnowAngel: so, ladies. on doug—or on the male of yr choice—what should be underneath?

|  | yes | no |
|---|---|---|
| boxers | 👍 | 👎 |
| tightie whities | 👍 | 👎 |
| jock straps | 👍 | 👎 |
| man thongs | 👍 | 👎 |
| undershirts | 👍 | 👎 |
| wife-beaters | 👍 | 👎 |

zoegirl: shld undershirts show? what do u think? and wife-beaters? anyone voting for a name-change on that one, say "aye."

Send     Cancel

86

zoegirl:      i mean what kind of guy wld wear something called a wife-beater?

**mad maddie: u can't think about it literally. it's just slang, zoe.**

SnowAngel:    but she's right, the term's gross. besides, it makes me think of pit stains.

**mad maddie: which btw r totally hot!**

SnowAngel:    *rolls eyes*

SnowAngel:    hot like ian's Bernie Mac t-shirt? *tactfully presses Abercrombie & Fitch gift card into maddie's hand*

zoegirl:      moving on . . . what should be on top:

|  | yes | no |
|---|---|---|
| t-shirts | 👍 | 👎 |
| button-downs | 👍 | 👎 |
| flannel shirts | 👍 | 👎 |
| striped shirts | 👍 | 👎 |
| hawaiian shirts | 👍 | 👎 |
| vintage shirts | 👍 | 👎 |
| hoodies | 👍 | 👎 |
| crew necks | 👍 | 👎 |
| v-necks | 👍 | 👎 |

Send     Cancel

| | | yes | no |
|---|---|:---:|:---:|

**mad maddie:** **serious question**
SnowAngel: but not S-E-R-I-O-U-S serious. just serious-ish.
**mad maddie:** **how do we feel about v-necks?**
zoegirl: and, um, hairy chests?

| | yes | no |
|---|:---:|:---:|
| scarves | ☺ | ☹ |
| bowties | ☺ | ☹ |
| neckties | ☺ | ☹ |
| ascots | ☺ | ☹ |
| bling | ☺ | ☹ |

zoegirl: bling? did someone just say . . . bling?!
**mad maddie:** **yeah. youse gotta problem with dat?**
SnowAngel: *shudders*
SnowAngel: we're skipping bling. unless u like bling. but i'd much rather discuss vests, k?

| | yes | no |
|---|:---:|:---:|
| vests | ☺ | ☹ |
| blazers | ☺ | ☹ |
| jean jackets | ☺ | ☹ |
| leather jackets | ☺ | ☹ |

Send   Cancel

down jackets 👍 👎

SnowAngel: so what's on the bottom?
**mad maddie: the rear! the fanny! the boo-tocks! and—ahem—the "flip side," shall we say?!**
SnowAngel: be honest. do u notice a guy's package?
zoegirl: no, and i certainly don't use the term "package." and neither shld u.
**mad maddie: a related philosophical question: do butts matter?**
zoegirl: or more importantly, do pants make the butt? or do butts make the pants?
**mad maddie: i guess that depends on the butt. is the butt a non-butt, a pancake butt—as in wide and round—a muscular soccer player butt, a round butt?**

|  | yes | no |
|---|---|---|
| khakis | 👍 | 👎 |
| cords | 👍 | 👎 |
| Levi's | 👍 | 👎 |
| baggy jeans | 👍 | 👎 |
| girl jeans | 👍 | 👎 |
| emo jeans | 👍 | 👎 |

zoegirl: another serious-ish question. how low shld a guy's jeans hang?

Send  Cancel

| | |
|---|---|
| **mad maddie:** | **well, lower than the WAIST, i'd say** |
| SnowAngel: | forget the jeans! how about a kilt? |
| zoegirl: | is it true what they say? about what a guy wears under a kilt? |
| **mad maddie:** | **oh yes. trust me.** |

|  | yes | no |
|---|---|---|
| kilts | 😊 | 😒 |

| | |
|---|---|
| zoegirl: | i woke up this morning wondering if doug will go bald. |
| **mad maddie:** | **it depends. is his mother's father bald?** |
| **mad maddie:** | **if so, he prolly will. sorry, charlie. maybe we should move on to . . . toupees?** |
| zoegirl: | or hats? |

|  | yes | no |
|---|---|---|
| baseball cap | 😊 | 😒 |

| | |
|---|---|
| SnowAngel: | and in terms of baseball caps, what do u think, frontward or backward? |
| zoegirl: | i think backward is cute. |

|  | yes | no |
|---|---|---|
| knit or skull cap | 😊 | 😒 |
| fifties-style Havana fedora | 😊 | 😒 |

| | |
|---|---|
| SnowAngel: | and last but not least, what about overall style? what's yr preference? |

90

| | yes | no |
|---|---|---|
| gangsta | 👍 | 👎 |
| goth | 👍 | 👎 |
| preppy | 👍 | 👎 |
| punk | 👍 | 👎 |
| classic rocker | 👍 | 👎 |
| metrosexual | 👍 | 👎 |
| sk8r | 👍 | 👎 |
| arty | 👍 | 👎 |
| rasta | 👍 | 👎 |
| sporty | 👍 | 👎 |
| brit | 👍 | 👎 |
| euro | 👍 | 👎 |
| emo | 👍 | 👎 |
| nerdy guy | 👍 | 👎 |

**mad maddie:  all-righty, then! we've solved the world's problems!**

Send    Cancel

# bff

## wishful thinking . . .
### dress yr guy

zoegirl:     i love my doug, u know i do. but sometimes i fantasize about giving him a makeover. is that bad?

**mad maddie:  dude, of course not.**

SnowAngel:  i think all girls do that.

SnowAngel:  *shields eyes with hand and looks out at dear darling bff's* y'all do, right? so spill!

**mad maddie:  ur at a club waiting for yr guy to arrive. he shows up looking totally hot. what's he got on?**

_____

_____

_____

_____

_____

zoegirl:     yr guy needs to look sharp for yr cousin's wedding—and it's the first time yr family's meeting him (yikes!). what should he wear?

_____

_____

_____

_____

_____

Send      Cancel

# quiz
## is he right 4 u?

SnowAngel:  ok, brace yrself, cuz this cld hurt. i mean, hopefully it won't . . . but it cld.

SnowAngel:  u think yr romance is poy-fect, but yr bff's aren't convinced. 😗

zoegirl:  take this quiz as an honest way of seeing if they might be onto something!!!

1. kissing him . . .
   a. feels so right!!
   b. makes * the * earth * move * under * yr * feet *
   c. is, like, a nonevent.

2. u borrow yr guy's iPod, and realize that his playlist . . .
   a. is loaded with music u've never heard before— some rocks and some sucks.
   b. is loaded with music u can't stand.
   c. includes all yr faves.

3. u and yr guy r making plans for Friday night. u . . .
   a. both want to do the same thing! 😊
   b. feel like u kinda hafta do what he wants to do.
   c. want to do totally utterly different things. the two of u get into an argument about it and u sulk, cry, storm off, or all of the above.

Send    Cancel

4. ur forced by yr parents to spend a week visiting relatives in nowheres-ville. yr guy . . .
   a. figures the 2 of u can catch up when ur back in town.
   b. IMs and texts u every day while ur away. man, he misses u!
   c. only checks in with u once but u weren't expecting to hear from him anyway.

5. ur at a party with yr guy's friends from summer camp, none of whom u've met before. he . . .
   a. is obviously the big fish in his own small pond. u admire his popularity from a chair in the corner.
   b. flirts with his friend's big sister. she's hot!
   c. introduces u to everyone and keeps u laughing all night.

6. yr mom invites yr guy to join yr family for dinner. he . . .
   a. is an hour late. but he enjoys the meal. with a little ketchup, everything tastes great!
   b. shows up with flowers and charms everyone with his sense of humor and genuine appreciation for yr dad's cooking.
   c. sneaks a couple of beers before heading over. ("man, mrs. smith, the service here is better than at hooters!")

7. ur unsure of the new dress u bought for the dance. yr guy . . .

Send    Cancel

a. rolls his eyes and tells u the dress makes yr butt look huge.

b. tells u over and over how beautiful u look. hubba hubba!

c. suggests u stop worrying. u'd look great in anything—and even better in nothing at all!

8. it's yr birthday! yr guy . . .

   a. writes u a poem and gives u a bouquet of flowers he picked himself.

   b. forgets it entirely.

   c. gives u a signed copy of his band's new demo CD.

9. u and yr guy r at a party and u've got to get home. he . . .

   a. complains that ur holding him back. this party is raging and he's *not* leaving!

   b. gets yr coat and his, and the 2 of u r out the door.

   c. bribes yr bff to drive u home. the party's just heating up!

10. yr friend natalie just broke up with her boyfriend. it's Saturday night, and she's home by herself. ur worried about her. yr guy . . .

    a. asks her out on what he calls a "sympathy date."

    b. offers to take u both out for ice cream.

    c. tells u he thinks she was too bossy for her own good.

# quiz results!

1: a = 😊, b = 😵, c = 😕; 2: a = 😵, b = 😕, c = 😊;
3: a = 😊, b = 😵, c = 😕; 4: a = 😕, b = 😊, c = 😵;
5: a = 😵, b = 😕, c = 😊; 6: a = 😵, b = 😊, c = 😕;
7: a = 😕, b = 😊, c = 😵; 8: a = 😊, b = 😕, c = 😵;
9: a = 😕, b = 😊, c = 😵; 10: a = 😵, b = 😊, c = 😕.

Name: _____     Name: _____

😊: ____  😵: ____  😕: ____     😊: ____  😵: ____  😕: ____

Name: _____     Name: _____

😊: ____  😵: ____  😕: ____     😊: ____  😵: ____  😕: ____

zoegirl:     if u chose mostly 😊's, u've got a keeper! yr guy is
             sweet, sexy, romantic—he's got it all (and he's yrs!).

SnowAngel:   if u chose mostly 😵's, uh-oh, u've got trouble with
             a capital T! he may be worth the effort u put in, but
             watch yrself—heartbreak cld be around the corner.

**mad maddie:   if u chose mostly 😕's, yr guy's a hopeless case! time
             to move on. there r plenty of other prospects out there
             who r better than this loser!**

96

# yr bff flicklist

## date movies

SnowAngel: i'm asking rob out to the movies and i want it to b romantic beyond belief. any suggestions?

**mad maddie: good luck. he'll think the Transformers movie is a good date flick.**

zoegirl: that's the problem! guys don't even \*have\* date movie radar. but maybe they say the same thing about us!

SnowAngel: ok, bff's, let's make a list of date movies.

zoegirl: first list the flicks that r totally romantic.

**madmaddie: then list the flicks that yr dates or crushes (or brothers, or guy friends, etc., etc., etc.) insist r GREAT date movies.**

SnowAngel: and last, come up with some surefire guy-friendly flicks that would make both u and yr date happy

**madmaddie: and in the mood for . . . who knows what!**

swoon-worthies

_____

_____

_____

_____

_____

_____

Send    Cancel

guy-worthies

_____

_____

_____

_____

_____

_____

guy-friendly

_____

_____

_____

_____

_____

_____

**mad maddie:** **when in doubt, i say pick a comedy**

zoegirl: good idea. when u giggle, u feel more relaxed. more yrself.

SnowAngel: no no no, u sillies. when in doubt, pick a scary movie! then u get to squeal and grab his arm!!!!

**mad maddie:** **what if he squeals and grabs yr arm?**

SnowAngel: uh . . . hmm.

SnowAngel: make sure ur with the right guy and not his 4-yr-old little brother? 😁

Send     Cancel

# top 5 . . .
## pressies a guy can give a girl for valentine's day

**mad maddie:** **not that he'd call them "pressies," of course**

SnowAngel: well, he might. if he was all metro and had a mustache and thought deep thoughts in the dark of the night . . .

**mad maddie:** **i so shouldn't have told y'all about that . . .**

SnowAngel: sweetheart, u shld tell us *everything*. surely u know that by now!

zoegirl: presents! we're supposed to be discussing presents!

SnowAngel: *looks dreamily off into the past* i remember, back when i was wee, receiving a vair vair lovely v-day pressie.

SnowAngel: i called it "jeepy-poo," and it slept beside me on my pillow . . .

**mad maddie:** **ok, yeah. jeep, um, trumps pretty much everything. but not every guy is going to give a girl a jeep . . .**

zoegirl: nor is every girl going to KEEP THE JEEP once she looks into her own heart and realizes how unfair it wld be to accept something like that from a guy she doesn't actually love.

SnowAngel: *pouts*

zoegirl: but a jeep, tho not to keep, is still better than being given . . . uh . . . a bighorn sheep!

**mad maddie:** **was that a poem? that was a really horrible poem, zo.**

SnowAngel: yeah, leave the poem-ing to doug, cupcake.

SnowAngel: however, i wld like to suggest that a poem—

Send    Cancel

**mad maddie:** a good poem

SnowAngel: —*is* a sweet v-day gift.

**mad maddie:** now list five other mega-awesome, ultra-fabulous
v-day presents, k? the only rule: NO BIGHORN SHEEP!

1. _____

2. _____

3. _____

4. _____

5. _____

### time out for . . .
# u and yr panis

SnowAngel: Erma Bombeck: "When humor goes, there goes
civilization . . ."

**mad maddie:** with. my. panis. omg.

**mad maddie:** come back, civilization! come back, panis!!!

Send    Cancel

# top 10 ways to tell . . .
## a guy's a player

SnowAngel: i dated a player once. *makes eyes go slitty* rob tyler.

**mad maddie: dude who cheated on u? over an awesome blossom? tsk, tsk.**

SnowAngel: he took tonnie wyndham on a date to chili's! AND I SAW THEM WITH MY MOM AND CHRISSY!!!

**mad maddie: angela! u never told us that part—about how yr mom and chrissy were with the two-timing bastard, too!!!!**

SnowAngel: haha. *I* was with mom and chrissy. *he* was with THE EVIL ONE!

zoegirl: except wasn't rob the evil one, really?

**mad maddie: who's more evil—the guy who cheats on his girlfriend, or the girl he cheats with?**

zoegirl: excellent question. talk about that as u rank the following warning signs, giving a "1" to the most telltale player indicator and a "10" to the least.

SnowAngel: do it with yr bff's! and then have a nice little chat about players u've known, players u suspect, and how to run like heck when u c one snapping his fingers and coming yr way.

SnowAngel: oh, and please feel free to say "playa" instead of "player" if ya want!

\_\_\_\_ he gives u—and every other girl he meets—a lot of attention.

\_\_\_\_ he often wants to do things u don't want to do.

_____ a girl who isn't his sister answers his cell phone.

_____ yr parents don't like him.

_____ u might text or IM him and not hear back from him for days.

_____ he's had lots and lots AND LOTS of girlfriends.

_____ he spends more time checking himself out in a mirror than anyone u know.

_____ he doesn't like yr friends.

_____ he borrows money and keeps saying he'll pay it back.

_____ he asks u to do an assignment for him because "ur soooo much better than me in [fill in yr best subject here, dear reader!]."

**mad maddie:   add you own signs if ours don't make yr top ten . . .**

___ _____

___ _____

___ _____

___ _____

___ _____

Send     Cancel

# ☺ **serious conversation time** ☺
## two-timing

| | |
|---|---|
| SnowAngel: | that's right, folks! it's time to talk about SOMETHING DEPRESSING again! |
| zoegirl: | oh, angela. it doesn't *have* to be depressing. |
| **mad maddie:** | **bull-pooty. there is no situation in which two-timing isn't depressing.** |
| zoegirl: | unless it helps u realize that ur with the wrong guy . . . |
| **mad maddie:** | **whatevs. bff's: u c yr friend's guy out with another girl, and it's clear that A DALLIANCE is going on.** |
| SnowAngel: | "dalliance"! mads, nice! |
| **mad maddie:** | **what do u do?** |

_____

_____

_____

_____

_____

_____

_____

_____

_____

_____

_____

Send    Cancel

# top 5 . . .
## suckiest presents a guy can
## give a girl for valentine's day

| | |
|---|---|
| zoegirl: | we've talked about best-ever v-day presents. now let's talk about worst! |
| SnowAngel: | *hits game show dinger* worsted wool! |
| **mad maddie:** | **ha! excellent! worsted wool wld indeed be a present made of suckiness. good one, a!** |
| SnowAngel: | ☺ thk u, sweetie |
| SnowAngel: | i don't even know what "worsted wool" is, to tell the truth. zo said "worst" and i just went from there. |
| zoegirl: | ok, worsted wool. i'll take that. now list others! |
| **mad maddie:** | **think of real life examples, like—ahem—the barnes & noble gift certificate a certain someone gave another certain someone . . .** |
| SnowAngel: | oh, that was bad, i admit. |
| zoegirl: | yeahhhhhh . . . especially since he gave u a JEEP. |
| SnowAngel: | but that was el crapito pressie from girl to guy. we want el crappito pressie from guy to girl. do it to it, dahlinks! |

1. _____

2. _____

3. _____

4. _____

5. _____

# ☺ **serious conversation time** ☺
## two-timing, part two

SnowAngel: ok, follow-up to our last depressing—i mean serious—convo. say yr boyfriend \*does\* cheat on u, but he says he's soooooo sorry and he grovels and all that.

SnowAngel: do u give him a 2nd chance?

zoegirl: and u can't just say "yes" or "no."

**mad maddie: well, u can, but we will be disappointed in u.**

SnowAngel: it's a complicated question. it deserves a complicated answer!

Send    Cancel

# yr bff playlist
## for breakups and other sad times

zoegirl:      do y'all know that the chinese word for "crisis" is made up of 2 characters: danger + opportunity?

**mad maddie:** **no way. cool!**

zoegirl:      doug learned that during his semester at sea.

SnowAngel:      that's an excellent thing to remind yrself of when ur dealing with A BREAKUP. yeah, it sucks, but yeah, it opens yr life to new opportunities, 2.

**mad maddie:** **something else that's good to remind yrself of when/if u have to deal with a breakup? IF THE GUY DOESN'T WANT TO BE WITH U, THEN GUESS WHAT? U DON'T WANT TO BE WITH HIM, EITHER.**

SnowAngel:      even if u think u do. cuz if he's just not that into u or whatever, then u can drive yrself crazy trying to make him be, but (a) it's never gonna work and (b) why wld u do that, anyway? why go begging and chasing a guy who doesn't appreciate the wonderfulness that is U?!!!

zoegirl:      one thing that happens a lot, i think, is that a girl—and i'm not naming names here—sometimes creates this vision of who the guy could be and gets fixated on that, instead of accepting the truth of who he really is.

**mad maddie:** **i second that.**

SnowAngel:      i also think that sometimes girls—and yes, i count myself in this category tho i'm trying to do better— try to convince themselves for waaaaaay too long that a guy can CHANGE. like my aunt sadie says, "the first time a guy shows u who he is? believe him."

Send      Cancel

**mad maddie:** **ooo, that's a nice way to put it.**

SnowAngel: upshot: breakups r going to happen . . . and they will suck.

**mad maddie:** **even if it's for the best, it'll still suck when ur in the middle of it.**

SnowAngel: which is why we need to put together a kick-booty breakup playlist now, with songs that let u cry—but also include power anthem songs like "since u've been gone," or "never again"

zoegirl: together with yr bff's, start writing down songs, and pass the list around till ur all happy with it.

SnowAngel: and if one of y'all goes thru a crappy breakup? THEN IT IS THE JOB OF THE OTHER BFF'S TO HIT THE "PLAY" BUTTON PRONTO!

Send    Cancel

# yr bff flicklist
## good cry movies

SnowAngel:   also good for breakups? good cry movies.

**mad maddie:**   **u and the crying. sheesh.**

SnowAngel:   it's . . . purgative!

zoegirl:   i don't think that's the word u mean. a "purgative" is, um, a laxative.

SnowAngel:   ewwww! 😜

SnowAngel:   but y'all know what i mean. a good tearjerker lets u get all the yucky sadness out.

**mad maddie:**   **which IS like a purgative, if u use a little creative thinking . . .**

zoegirl:   list time! best super-sad faves!

**mad maddie:**   **write 1 down, pass it around, 99 purgatives yet to be scrawled!**

_____

_____

_____

_____

_____

_____

_____

_____

_____

_____

Send     Cancel

# top 10 great things about . . .
## being single

SnowAngel:   *adjusts adorable newsboy cap jauntily on head*
SnowAngel:   let's do it, tigers! time to remember why it's great to be single!!!
**mad maddie:**   **score the following from greatest (1) to least great (10)**
SnowAngel:   add yr own perks to being a single gal, too
zoegirl:   then share share share with yr buds!
**mad maddie:**   **and do a fist-bump-explosion! YEAAHHHH!**

\_\_\_\_ u don't have to watch the action movie of the month (unless u want to)

\_\_\_\_ u don't have to feel guilty for making him wait while u try on, like, the hundredth pair of skinny jeans (or feel compelled to ask, "do these make my butt look big?")

\_\_\_\_ u don't have to hang around his locker, hoping he'll acknowledge u while he talks with his buddies

\_\_\_\_ u don't have to worry about burping or farting at the wrong time (bff's can handle anything, but romance is a fragile thing)

\_\_\_\_ u don't have to watch him sulk when u get yet another text from another guy who just happens to be one of yr bff's

___ u don't have to worry about whether u remembered to shave yr legs

___ u don't have to spend time on primping and perfecting yr amazing look (unless u want to)

___ u don't have to obsess about what ur giving him for Valentine's Day (too big? too little? too romantic? too much "ur-like-a-brother-to-me"?)

___ u can dress up, dress down—whatever floats *yr* boat, no one else's

___ u can be as flirty as u want to be

___ u can do what u want, when u want to (and with yr bff's!)

___ _____

___ _____

___ _____

___ _____

___ _____

___ _____

Send      Cancel

# ☺ serious conversation time ☺
## abusive boyfriend

**zoegirl:**  ok, we so don't want any of y'all to be in this situation, ever.

**mad maddie:** but bad things happen.

*SnowAngel:*  god, i'm getting sick of these "serious conversations."

**mad maddie:** hey. if u talk about hard stuff, then ur, like, more prepared to deal with hard stuff IF it ever comes up.

**zoegirl:**  so with that in mind . . . what wld u do if yr boyfriend hit u or said really mean things to u?

Send    Cancel

# another fun thing to do!
## make a cool plan!

**mad maddie:** **one of my best-ever memories was when y'all brought me that care package and left it at my front door, remember?**

**mad maddie:** **after the whole jana incident, at the frat house?**

SnowAngel: god, that seems so long ago. we were so young.

zoegirl: but u didn't even come out and, like, say anything to us, mads.

zoegirl: it really meant that much to u?

**mad maddie:** **uh, YES. and i didn't come out at the time, cuz at the time i was still nursing my wounds.**

**mad maddie:** **jana sent a picture of me, topless, to every single person at school. it takes a long time to get over that.**

zoegirl: um . . . true. point taken.

SnowAngel: i'm glad we made u feel better . . . even if u weren't able to be properly appreciative. *winks at maddie to show it's a tease*

**mad maddie:** **well, u did, and all bff's shld do the same when one of their own is hurting.**

**mad maddie:** **make a pre-emptive plan NOW, sez i. plan a grrl power sleepover or something, but don't actually call it grrl power cuz u will sound stupid.**

SnowAngel: oh, poo. grrl power isn't stupid. it's cute!

**mad maddie:** **deets to consider: who's hosting? who's bringing munchies? wha'cha gonna do to make it the best grrl power sleepover party ever?!**

zoegirl: first, organize the basics

Send    Cancel

when: _____

where: _____

who to invite: _____

_____

_____

_____

_____

_____

_____

_____

_____

_____

_____

_____

_____

SnowAngel:   come up with a theme!!!! me lub themes!!!!

_____

_____

_____

_____

Send     Cancel

**mad maddie:   i like lists. i admit it. so, some lists to get ya going:**

munchies to make or buy:

_____

_____

_____

_____

_____

games to play:

_____

_____

_____

_____

_____

other activities:

_____

_____

_____

_____

_____

Send      Cancel

SnowAngel:    now design yr invite here:

Send     Cancel

# yr bff playlist
## grrl power

| | |
|---|---|
| **mad maddie:** | **don't forget THE TUNES part of grrl power nite** |
| SnowAngel: | mads, do u realize u've kinda taken on the whole grrl power thing? i mean, i'm just wondering . . . |
| zoegirl: | make fun of something long enuff and it STICKS, hee hee |
| **mad maddie:** | **oh god** |
| **mad maddie:** | **this is terrible** |
| SnowAngel: | no, it's not. it's grrl-power-lectable! *puts hand to mouth and giggles* |
| zoegirl: | ur right about needing tunes, tho. so bring it home, mads! tell 'em what they need to do! |
| **mad maddie:** | **make a grrl power playlist** |
| **mad maddie:** | **(and i said that fully in a monotone, just fyi. and now am off to hypnosis therapy . . .)** |

# yr bff flicklist
## grrl power

zoegirl: while mads is off at hypno-therapy, let's do more grrl power stuff to surprise her with when she comes back!

SnowAngel: YES! *smooches her zo*

SnowAngel: movies? grrl power flicks of awesomeness?

zoegirl: yeah yeah yeah! with, like, some romantic comedies, but not all romantic comedies. include . . . well, not to be bossy. . . but i personally think y'all shld include some classics like *Thelma and Louise*, and maybe a rockin' indie like *Little Miss Sunshine*.

SnowAngel: plus just all the cheesy delites that yr boy-type-peeps might scoff at.

SnowAngel: and for super grrl powers, add freeze-frame-worthy moments after the movie's title. and whatever u do . . . don't forget the popcorn!

Send Cancel

# yr opinion
## lingerie

SnowAngel:     *smiles brightly*

SnowAngel:     hello, mads. so glad u cld join us! we're gonna talk about grrl power lingerie now!

**mad maddie:** **ok, bye. walking back outta here.**

SnowAngel:     KIDDING!

zoegirl:     we r gonna talk about . . . undergarments, but we can let the grrl power bit drop.

zoegirl:     especially since some of them r so very NOT grrl power . . .

SnowAngel:     *widens eyes innocently* what, u don't consider granny panties the epitome of grrl power?

**mad maddie:** **i am feeling more grrrr power than grrl power. can we get on with the opinion-giving?!!!**

SnowAngel:     let's start with what's underneath:

|  | yes | no |
|---|---|---|
| thongs | 🙂👍 | 🙁👎 |
| boy shorts | 🙂👍 | 🙁👎 |
| briefs (granny panties) | 🙂👍 | 🙁👎 |
| bikini cut | 🙂👍 | 🙁👎 |
| French cut | 🙂👍 | 🙁👎 |
| _____ | 🙂👍 | 🙁👎 |

Send     Cancel

| | yes | no |
|---|---|---|
| _____ | 🙂👍 | 🙁👎 |
| _____ | 🙂👍 | 🙁👎 |
| _____ | 🙂👍 | 🙁👎 |

SnowAngel:   what about nylon versus cotton versus silk? we're
             talking BIG decision here, peeps.
**mad maddie:  cotton**
zoegirl:     cotton
SnowAngel:   silk!!!!!
zoegirl:     and the other big decisions . . .

| | yes | no |
|---|---|---|
| what about lace? | 🙂👍 | 🙁👎 |
| what about bows? | 🙂👍 | 🙁👎 |
| shld the word *juicy* ever appear anywhere near yr butt? | 🙂👍 | 🙁👎 |
| shld yr undies *ever* show? | 🙂👍 | 🙁👎 |
| what about crotchless panties? | 🙂👍 | 🙁👎 |
| shld u ever go commando? | 🙂👍 | 🙁👎 |
| _____ | 🙂👍 | 🙁👎 |
| _____ | 🙂👍 | 🙁👎 |

Send     Cancel

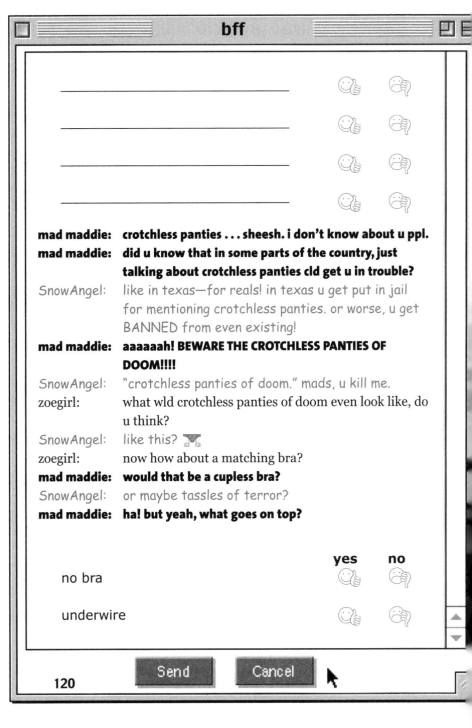

| | yes | no |
|---|---|---|
| _____ | ☺ | ☹ |
| _____ | ☺ | ☹ |
| _____ | ☺ | ☹ |
| _____ | ☺ | ☹ |

**mad maddie:** **crotchless panties . . . sheesh. i don't know about u ppl.**

**mad maddie:** **did u know that in some parts of the country, just talking about crotchless panties cld get u in trouble?**

SnowAngel: like in texas—for reals! in texas u get put in jail for mentioning crotchless panties. or worse, u get BANNED from even existing!

**mad maddie:** **aaaaaah! BEWARE THE CROTCHLESS PANTIES OF DOOM!!!!**

SnowAngel: "crotchless panties of doom." mads, u kill me.

zoegirl: what wld crotchless panties of doom even look like, do u think?

SnowAngel: like this? 🩲

zoegirl: now how about a matching bra?

**mad maddie:** **would that be a cupless bra?**

SnowAngel: or maybe tassles of terror?

**mad maddie:** **ha! but yeah, what goes on top?**

| | yes | no |
|---|---|---|
| no bra | ☺ | ☹ |
| underwire | ☺ | ☹ |

Send    Cancel

| racerback | 🙂👍 | 🙁👎 |
| --- | --- | --- |
| strapless | 🙂👍 | 🙁👎 |
| push-up | 🙂👍 | 🙁👎 |
| adhesive cups | 🙂👍 | 🙁👎 |
| gel | 🙂👍 | 🙁👎 |
| gel inserts | 🙂👍 | 🙁👎 |
| padded | 🙂👍 | 🙁👎 |

zoegirl: there r times when a padded bra is important. like, i wear a padded bra, but it isn't for the extra ummph, if u know what i mean. it's, um, to keep my nipples from poking out.

**mad maddie: nipple-itis. serious concern. i hear ya.**

SnowAngel: not that there's anything wrong with nipples . . .

SnowAngel: *glances around with interest* can we get banned for talking about nipples?

|  | **yes** | **no** |
| --- | --- | --- |
| is it OK for yr nipples to show? | 🙂👍 | 🙁👎 |
| is it OK for yr bra straps to show if they're pretty? | 🙂👍 | 🙁👎 |
| what if they're ugly? | 🙂👍 | 🙁👎 |

Send    Cancel

is it OK to wear a sports bra in public?

**mad maddie:** **did u see jana today? methinks her cups runneth over.**

SnowAngel: i TOLD her she shld get a bigger bra, but of course she took it the wrong way.

**mad maddie:** **that's what u call a bra faux pas, or *bra pas* for those of us in the know. yr turn. yes, U. Describe the biggest bra pas u've ever seen . . . or experienced.**

_____

_____

_____

_____

_____

_____

_____

_____

zoegirl: i have a bra invention. i haven't made it, but i want to.

zoegirl: it wld be: a nude-colored bra, but with straps that were light pink or purple, or something else pretty. u cld wear it under a tank top, and it wld be invisible-ish where it was supposed to be, but if the straps peeked out, they'd be cute instead of ugly!

SnowAngel: brilliant! now, y'all's turn. if u cld invent the perfect bra, what wld it look like? what features wld it have?

Send    Cancel

122

**mad maddie:**  **a built-in pocketknife, perchance?**

*SnowAngel:*  *ha ha, mads. always the jokester, ain'cha?*

zoegirl:  draw pics and write descriptions here!

Send    Cancel

# ☺ **serious conversation time** ☺
## birth control

**mad maddie:** one day, probably, u r going to have sex. i'm not saying today, or tomorrow, or next thursday. but one day it'll prolly happen. r u with me?

SnowAngel: no. they're freaking out and running. c?

**mad maddie:** nuh-uh, and if they r, tell 'em to come back. cuz when it comes to sex, it's just plain stupid to be all la-la-la, i'm in denial, la-la-la!

zoegirl: every girl is going to be different in terms of what she believes and where she is with the whole issue of sex. BUT. when u think about sex . . . how do u c yrself handling the birth control issue?

**mad maddie:** yeah. what's yer plan, ladies?

_____

_____

_____

_____

_____

_____

_____

_____

_____

_____

Send    Cancel

# check in with yr bff's

**zoegirl:** fill in the following about each other. like, if maddie and angela and i were the ones filling this out, angela might read out the first question, and then as a group we'd discuss what *each* bff's best quality is. then we'd write down what we came up with for each person. easy-peasy!

**SnowAngel:** yr best quality is . . .

_____

_____

_____

_____

**zoegirl:** what i admire about u is . . .

_____

_____

_____

_____

**mad maddie: a way i wish i could be more like u is . . .**

_____

_____

_____

_____

Send   Cancel

**bff**

SnowAngel:   a time when i really missed u was . . .

_____

_____

_____

_____

**mad maddie:  i always laugh when u . . .**

_____

_____

_____

_____

zoegirl:       u were there for me when u . . .

_____

_____

_____

_____

**mad maddie:  one thing u need to work on . . .**
SnowAngel:   *assumes a solemn air and raises right hand*
SnowAngel:   we, yr best buds, promise 2 NOT hate u 4-evah if u
                 tell us, so be honest.
zoegirl:       but gentle!

_____

126

Send    Cancel

SnowAngel: and last but not least, one thing u shld never change . . .

SnowAngel: *wipes tear from eye* awwww! big hug!!!!
zoegirl: big grrl power hug!
**mad maddie: big thwap-u-on-the-noggin, grrl!**
SnowAngel: run, zo! RUN!!!!!! 😨

## time out for . . .
## u and yr panis

SnowAngel: y'all know the wizard of oz, right? by l. frank baum? well, here's a two-fer: "Imagination led Columbus to discover America . . ."
**mad maddie: with my panis!**
SnowAngel: "Imagination led Franklin to discover electricity . . ."
**mad maddie: c'mon, zo. u know u wanna . . .**
zoegirl: oh, fine. Imagination led franklin to discover electricity . . . with my panis!

Send    Cancel

127

# ☺ **serious conversation time** ☺
## best qualities u offer as a friend

SnowAngel:    finally! a \*happy\* serious conversation!

**mad maddie:**    **pass out the Cheese Nips, baby!**

zoegirl:    y'all already talked about each other's best qualities.

**mad maddie:**    **now it's time to shine that lovin' flashlight at yr own sweet self. some ppl call it self-affirmation. me? i call it owning yr strengths.**

SnowAngel:    and believe us, each one of u has LOTS of 'em!

_____

_____

_____

_____

_____

_____

_____

_____

_____

_____

_____

_____

_____

Send    Cancel

# yr opinion
## slang for "penis"

| | |
|---|---|
| **mad maddie:** | **zo? cover yr ears.** |
| zoegirl: | why? |
| **mad maddie:** | **cuz i told u so** |
| **mad maddie:** | **AND cuz it's TIME TO DISCUSS MALE GENITALIA, oh yes it is** |
| SnowAngel: | can we get banned for this? |
| **mad maddie:** | **here's hoping!!!!!** |
| SnowAngel: | what's yr opinion? r the following terms ok or not ok? |

                                         **yes**    **no**

private parts

under what circumstances OK/not OK?

_____

_____

johnson

under what circumstances OK/not OK?

_____

_____

Send     Cancel

mini me
under what circumstances OK/not OK?

_____

_____

lizard

under what circumstances OK/not OK?

_____

_____

one-eyed trouser snake

under what circumstances OK/not OK?

_____

_____

schlong

under what circumstances OK/not OK?

_____

_____

peter

under what circumstances OK/not OK?

Send     Cancel

wiener

under what circumstances OK/not OK?

willy

under what circumstances OK/not OK?

**mad maddie:** **and what if the willy becomes a woody?**
zoegirl:      maddie!!!!!!
**mad maddie:** **i told u to cover yr ears.**
SnowAngel:   but seriously, if it's coming anywhere near u, then u
             need to put a condom on it. pronto.
**mad maddie:** **yes, sirree, put a hat on it.**
**mad maddie:** **and right away.**

Send    Cancel

# ☺ serious conversation time ☺

## sex

zoegirl:     so it's kinda public knowledge that doug and i have, u know, had sex.

SnowAngel:   *widens eyes and claps hand to mouth* ooooo! i'm telling!!!!!!

zoegirl:     but we took that step after a LOT of thought. it wasn't some random, spur-of-the-moment decision.

**mad maddie:**   **of course it wasn't.**

**mad maddie:**   **in fact, have u \*ever\* done anything random and spur-of-the-moment?**

zoegirl:     not the question. the question is this: how long do y'all think a girl shld wait before having sex? and, like, what different factors shld go into the equation?

**mad maddie:**   **angela? we're talking about \*sex\*, and zoe is using terms like "factors" and "equation."**

SnowAngel:   i know. she is hopeless. if only we cld be more like her, right? ☺

zoegirl:     factors! equation! u have 10 minutes, and yes, punctuation counts! (kidding!!!!!)

_____

_____

_____

_____

_____

_____

Send    Cancel

# yr opinion
## slang for "breasts"

**mad maddie:**   zo, cover yr ears again.

zoegirl:   no! i won't. i refuse!

**mad maddie:**   ok, fine. but don't say I didn't warn u . . .

SnowAngel:   mads, the girl strode thru the mall WITH MARSHMALLOWS TAPED TO HER NIPPLES. i think she can handle a little boob talk.

zoegirl:   mini-marshmallows. can we clarify that, plz?

zoegirl:   (omg, i am so blushing just remembering!!!!)

**mad maddie:**   so, the following: ok or not ok to use when describing bazoombas?

zoegirl:   (they really were mini-marshmallows. teeny-weeny mini-marshmallows!!!)

|  | yes | no |
|---|---|---|
| boobs | 🙂 | 🙁 |

under what circumstances OK/not OK?

_____

_____

|  | yes | no |
|---|---|---|
| the girls | 🙂 | 🙁 |

under what circumstances OK/not OK?

_____

_____

# bff

tits

under what circumstances OK/not OK?

_____

_____

ta-tas (and NOT as in ttfn!)

under what circumstances OK/not OK?

_____

_____

bosom

under what circumstances OK/not OK?

_____

_____

hooters

under what circumstances OK/not OK?

_____

_____

Send    Cancel

134

cantaloupes
(or whatever fruit floats yr boat)

under what circumstances OK/not OK?

_____

_____

knockers

under what circumstances OK/not OK?

_____

_____

top shelf

under what circumstances OK/not OK?

_____

_____

**mad maddie:  what about jugs?**

SnowAngel:  omg. maddie, u can't be serious. that is SO vulgar.

zoegirl:  no to jugs. let's just agree to that now.

# yr opinion
## slang for "vagina"

**mad maddie:** **once again, zo, i must ask u now to cover yr—**

zoegirl: NO! sheesh, mads. no. lemme guess, we're talking about vaginas next?

SnowAngel: *blushing like a delicate flower*

SnowAngel: i actually still get embarrassed at that one, even more than at penis. why is that, do u think?

**mad maddie:** **it's just a weird-sounding word. that doesn't mean the vagina itself is weird. au contraire!**

SnowAngel: eeee. I am struggling here, just so u know.

SnowAngel: i mean, i know ur right. i *know* u r. vaginas r . . . biology! they're just part of us, and nothing to feel weird about. (but sometimes i still do . . .)

**mad maddie:** **that's ok, u'll get better with practice. SO! the following terms, ok or not?**

|  | yes | no |
|---|---|---|
| privates | 👍 | 👎 |

under what circumstances OK/not OK?

_____

_____

|  | yes | no |
|---|---|---|
| hoo-ha | 👍 | 👎 |

under what circumstances OK/not OK?

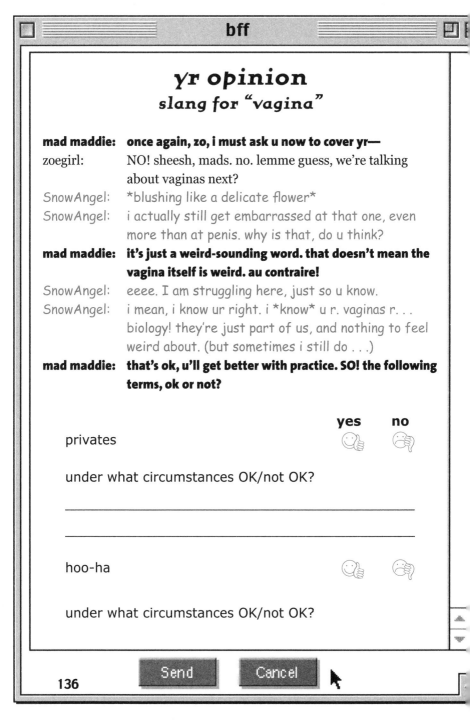

Send    Cancel

---

rhymes with Carolina

under what circumstances OK/not OK?

---

girl parts

under what circumstances OK/not OK?

---

va-jay-jay

under what circumstances OK/not OK?

---

netherlips

under what circumstances OK/not OK?

---

Send    Cancel

coochie

under what circumstances OK/not OK?

_____

_____

yoni

under what circumstances OK/not OK?

_____

_____

**mad maddie:** **btw, yes, there r some fully derogatory terms for this bit of anatomy that we will not even mention, thank u very much.**

zoegirl:     gross, wrong, yuck, and if a guy uses such a term?

**mad maddie:** **turn on yr heels and march yr va-jay-jay into the sunset, away from that low-life.**

SnowAngel:   and show some attitude, of course!

SnowAngel:   *does fancy hand-snappin' beyonce move*

Send    Cancel

# ☺ serious conversation time ☹
## pregnant friend

**SnowAngel:** u think it cld never happen to u, don'cha?

**mad maddie:** **cough cough—\*bristol palin\*—cough cough**

**zoegirl:** don't make fun of bristol palin. i think she's handling it with a lot of grace, i really do.

**SnowAngel:** u prolly think it cld never happen to one of yr friends, either.

**SnowAngel:** but what if it did? 😨

**SnowAngel:** what wld u do if one of yr friends told u SHE WAS PREGGERS?!!!!!

# yr you-ness

zoegirl:     remember when u were feeling all down on yrself? and
             feeling like u needed me & mads in order to be whole?
SnowAngel:   I *do* need u and mads in order to be whole!
zoegirl:     well . . . we r all part of each other, sure. and so so so so
             SO important, as all bff's r. BUT, i will say again what
             i said then: i don't give u your you-ness. u give *yrself*
             yr you-ness.
SnowAngel:   "you-ness." now there's a word for ya . . .
SnowAngel:   bff's, what makes u U?
**mad maddie:  yeah, like what about u makes u feel proud and
             confident?**
zoegirl:     make a list of what u think r yr best qualities. u can
             include character traits, physical stuff, attitudes . . .
             whatever.
SnowAngel:   but NO FAIR leaving it blank or writing "nothing" in
             sad little letters!!!! or i will have to come and do an
             intervention, cuz u KNOW u have many wonderful
             you-ness qualities that help shine light on this
             wonderful world of ours!!!! 🕯

Name: _____

_____

_____

_____

Name: _____

Send    Cancel

140

---

---

---

Name: _____

---

---

---

Name: _____

---

---

---

zoegirl:       now make a list of what u think gives each of yr bff's
               her own special "her-ness."

**mad maddie:   not to be confused with "harness."**

zoegirl:       no, and really, maddie, I don't think there was any
               confusion on that point.

**mad maddie:   just sayin' . . .**

SnowAngel:     what r yr darling bff's best qualities, features,
               etc.? yes, we touched on this earlier, but there can
               never be too much bff-loving. now u get to add all
               the stuff u didn't have space for. ☺

Send    Cancel

bff's name: _____

_____

_____

_____

bff's name: _____

_____

_____

_____

bff's name: _____

_____

_____

_____

bff's name: _____

_____

_____

_____

Send    Cancel

# yr opinion
## makeup

| | |
|---|---|
| SnowAngel: | oh, ladies, my ladies. please to excuse me while i go powder my nose. |
| **mad maddie:** | **translate: while she goes and pees like a racehorse.** |
| SnowAngel: | 😮 |
| SnowAngel: | nooooo, i really do need to powder my nose! It tends to get . . . a sheen about it, u c. and so . . . yeah. back in a flash! |
| zoegirl: | mads, ur the least makeup-y of all of us. why is that? |
| **mad maddie:** | **i dunno, just think it's dumb, mainly** |
| **mad maddie:** | **plus i suck at it . . .** |
| zoegirl: | about y'all, bff's? wanna weigh in? |
| zoegirl: | now let's start with foundation. |

|            | yes | no |
|------------|-----|-----|
| powder     | 🙂  | 🙁  |
| liquid     | 🙂  | 🙁  |
| mineral    | 🙂  | 🙁  |
| pancake    | 🙂  | 🙁  |
| blush      | 🙂  | 🙁  |
| au naturel | 🙂  | 🙁  |

143

| | | yes | no |
|---|---|---|---|
| SnowAngel: | i'm ba-a-a-ack! d'ya miss me? and more importantly: do i look less shiny? | | |
| **mad maddie:** | **u look boo-tee-ful, a. boo-tee-ful.** | | |
| SnowAngel: | *looks suspiciously at mads* | | |
| SnowAngel: | hmm. i sense suck-up-age. zo? was maddie bad-mouthing makeup again and saying it was dumb? | | |
| zoegirl: | uh . . . what she was saying, actually, was that it's time to weigh in on eye makeup! take it away, a! | | |
| SnowAngel: | ooo, with pleasure. | | |
| SnowAngel: | pretty pleez weigh in on eyes. | | |

| | yes | no |
|---|---|---|
| blue eye shadow | 😊 | 🙁 |
| eyebrow pencil | 😊 | 🙁 |
| eyebrow plucking or waxing | 😊 | 🙁 |
| eyeliner | 😊 | 🙁 |
| tinted eyelashes | 😊 | 🙁 |
| eyelash extensions | 😊 | 🙁 |

| | |
|---|---|
| SnowAngel: | lipstick time. but first, did I tell y'all about my new fave lipstick/lipgloss thingie? |
| zoegirl: | "lipstick" sounds like such a mom term. |
| SnowAngel: | yeah, i know. anyway, it's called "Sinner" and "Saint," and it's by Poppy, and actually they're 2 different lip color lines. u pick "sinner" if u want an opaque |

Send    Cancel

version of the color, and u pick "saint" if u want a
translucent version. i love it!!!! so cool!!!!

**mad maddie: which one r u, sinner or saint?**

SnowAngel: *says "tee-hee-hee" coquettishly*

SnowAngel: what do u think, sugar lump? AND what do u think
about lipstick in general?

| | yes | no |
|---|---|---|
| lipstick | 👍 | 👎 |
| gloss | 👍 | 👎 |
| bright red lipstick | 👍 | 👎 |
| coral lipstick | 👍 | 👎 |
| lip liner | 👍 | 👎 |
| lip plumper | 👍 | 👎 |

**mad maddie: there r other beauty-ish things to discuss, so let's go on
and get it over with.**

SnowAngel: mads, u r all bark and no bite when it comes to
beauty products. i mean, seriously. u don't dislike
makeup; ur just afraid of it.

**mad maddie: erm . . .**

SnowAngel: but I will help u!!!! don't u worry!!!!! I WILL GIVE U
THE MAKEOVER OF THE CENTURY! *😄*

**mad maddie: ok, I wasn't worried . . . but now i am!**

**mad maddie: tell me what u think of the following.**

Send    Cancel

|                         | **yes** | **no** |
|-------------------------|---------|--------|
| teeth whitener          | 🙂👍    | 🙁👎   |
| self-tanning creams     | 🙂👍    | 🙁👎   |
| bronzer                 | 🙂👍    | 🙁👎   |
| patchouli               | 🙂👍    | 🙁👎   |
| musk-scented perfume    | 🙂👍    | 🙁👎   |
| floral-scented perfume  | 🙂👍    | 🙁👎   |

### time out for . . .

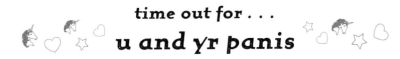

# u and yr panis

| zoegirl: | all right, angela. this one's for u. |
|----------|--------------------------------------|
| SnowAngel: | ur joining in! *happy dance, happy dance* |
| SnowAngel: | *waits eagerly* yessss? |
| zoegirl: | it's from Boethius. do u know who Boethius is? |
| SnowAngel: | nope, and don't care. *waits eagerly* |
| zoegirl: | he's a philosopher from the middle ages. "A man content to go to heaven alone will never go to heaven . . ." |
| SnowAngel: | WITH MY PANIS! and ain't THAT the truth, mister!!!! |
| **mad maddie:** | **good one, zo!** |

Send     Cancel

# another fun thing to do!
## give maddie—or yr bff—a makeover!!!!!!

SnowAngel: let's play pretend, shall we? let's say that maddie (or yr bff) has a first date with her big crush, and she wants to look casual but great. what look will make her sparkle inside and out?

_____

_____

_____

_____

_____

_____

SnowAngel: now maddie (or yr bff) is newly single and wants to bedazzle the available guys at yr cousin's wedding. what look will bring out her best?

_____

_____

_____

_____

_____

_____

147

SnowAngel:   and what if maddie (or yr bff) is going to a
             new school in the fall. what shld she do to look
             confident, radiant, and her very best on her first
             day?

_____

_____

_____

_____

_____

_____

**mad maddie:   angela? if i didn't love u so much?**
SnowAngel:   *pats madikins on her newly coiffed head*
SnowAngel:   but u do! so just enjoy yr new look. u look
             mahvelous, dahling! Simply mahvelous!!!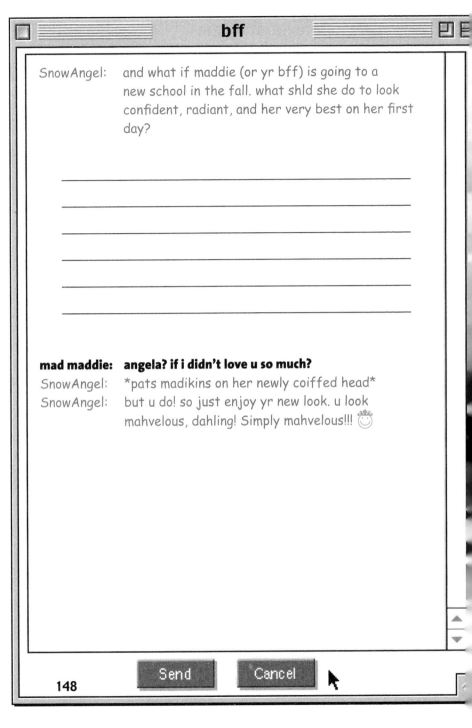

Send    Cancel

# quiz
## yr look

zoegirl: what's yr look? r u preppy or more of a country girl? glam or goth? artsy or athletic?

**mad maddie: how about slob?**

SnowAngel: take this quiz with yr bff's to find out!

1. which color combo is totally u?
   a. pink and green
   b. red and purple
   c. red and white
   d. silver and gold
   e. black and purple
   f. tan and blue (jeans that is)

2. congratulations! it's a girl! what do u name yr new sweet pea?
   a. Summer
   b. Kate
   c. Ratz
   d. Lola
   e. Emmy
   f. Charlotte

3. which of the following best describes yr new top?
   a. embroidered silk
   b. black velvet
   c. merino wool
   d. cotton

e.  snake skin

f.  fleece

4.  ur getting a tattoo! what r u getting inked?
    a.  a horseshoe on yr shlder
    b.  whatever Kate Moss has
    c.  omg, u wld never get a tattoo!
    d.  a lightning bolt on yr ankle
    e.  a spider web across yr back
    f.  a butterfly on yr shlder blade

5.  school's out for the year! what's yr dream summer job?
    a.  ur working in a funky coffee shop.
    b.  ur a nanny.
    c.  ur a retail associate at a couture jeans store.
    d.  ur a receptionist at a morgue.
    e.  ur a counselor at a soccer camp for girls.
    f.  ur working at a farm stand by day and on the rodeo circuit at night.

6.  u've given in to yr bad-girl urges. what do u do?
    a.  u bite a guy's neck at midnight.
    b.  u don't study for yr final exam.
    c.  u run away with a cowboy.
    d.  u "borrow" the team van to take yr pals to the beach for a moonlight swim.
    e.  u shoplift a bottle of Chanel No. 5.
    f.  u smoke pot with yr friend Dune.

7.  yr bff has given u a magazine subscription for Christmas. what is it?

Send   Cancel

a. I.M. Cowgirl
b. Art in America
c. Town & Country
d. Self
e. Gothic Beauty
f. W

8. it's Friday night, what r yr plans?
   a. a pizza party and bowling
   b. the steampunk convention
   c. a teen mixer at yr parents' club
   d. a gallery opening then a poetry reading
   e. the season's hottest runway show
   f. two-stepping with yr beau

9. how do u like getting wherever it is ur going?
   a. in a Volvo station wagon
   b. in a minivan—it holds the whole team
   c. in a vintage VW bus
   d. in a red convertible
   e. on a horse
   f. in a hearse

10. time for bed! what r u wearing?
    a. yr birthday suit!
    b. a ruffly Laura Ashley nightgown
    c. a black corset and black lace panties
    d. boy shorts and yr favorite team's t-shirt
    e. cowboy boots and a red bandanna
    f. a satin and chiffon babydoll slip with an empire waist

Send    Cancel

# *quiz results!*

1: (a) preppy, (b) artsy, (c) sporty, (d) glam, (e) goth,
(f) country girl; 2: (a) artsy, (b) sporty, (c) goth, (d) glam,
(e) country girl, (f) preppy; 3: (a) artsy, (b) glam, (c) preppy,
(d) country girl, (e) goth, (f) sporty; 4: (a) country girl,
(b) glam, (c) preppy, (d) sporty, (e) goth, (f) artsy;
5: (a) artsy, (b) preppy, (c) glam, (d) goth, (e) sporty,
(f) country girl; 6: (a) goth, (b) preppy, (c) country girl,
(d) sporty, (e) glam, (f) artsy; 7: (a) country girl, (b) artsy,
(c) preppy, (d) sporty, (e) goth, (f) glam; 8: (a) sporty,
(b) goth, (c) preppy, (d) artsy, (e) glam, (f) country girl;
9: (a) preppy, (b) sporty, (c) artsy, (d) glam, (e) country girl,
(f) goth; 10: (a) artsy, (b) preppy, (c) goth, (d) sporty,
(e) country girl, (f) glam

Name: _____

preppy: _____ artsy: _____ sporty: _____

glam: _____ goth: _____ c. girl: _____


Name: _____

preppy: _____ artsy: _____ sporty: _____

glam: _____ goth: _____ c. girl: _____


Name: _____

preppy: _____ artsy: _____ sporty: _____

Send     Cancel

152

glam: _____ goth: _____ c. girl: _____

Name: _____

preppy: _____ artsy: _____ sporty: _____

glam: _____ goth: _____ c. girl: _____

zoegirl:   so what's yr look? is it clear or r u a combination?
SnowAngel:  read below to find out more!

if ur **preppy**, u require only a few basics: a classic pearl neck-lace, a cashmere sweater set, and ribbon hair bands. but whatever u wear, yr look is put together but never fussy. any monograms r proudly displayed because yr family is important to u. though u might appear snobbish on the surface, u always make everyone feel welcome—ur a class act after all. a tradit-ionalist by nature, u luv to hang with yr tried-and-true bff's.

if ur **artsy**, whatever u wear expresses something about U. a beaded necklace u made yrself one day, a '70s miniskirt with purple clogs the next; u rn't afraid to mix and match. yr fashion finds—from yr secret awesome consignment shop, yr artist aunt's closet, or a fave sample sale—and yr eclectic style r the envy of yr friends. to some, yr look may be too offbeat. but to those who know u, ur just intense about the things that matter most to u: life, luv, creativity, and yr bff's!

if ur **sporty**, ur as comfortable with the funky two-tone-baseball-shirt-and-pinstripe look as u r with yr team's colors.

altho lots of people wear team names and numbers on their shirts as a fashion statement, for u, it's for real. whatever u wear, it's important that it's versatile as well as mad cool. highly competitive, u might forget everything but what it takes to be the best; however, yr loyal bff's will never forget yr big game . . . or let u forget the grrl power of teamwork.

if ur **glam**, whatever the "it" look is, baby, u've got it. from platform pumps to haute couture sneaks, from a diva 'do to a gold-lamé gown, it's not about the clothes, but how fab u look in them. yr style might bedazzle those who don't know u into thinking ur all surface, so sometimes u might need to let down yr sophisticated updo. No matter what, yr true-blue bff's know that yr fashion-forward thinking is just part of yr deep-down desire to make the world a better place.

if ur **goth**, yr clothes come in three colors: black, blacker, and blackest. u may accessorize with studded cuffs, a cape, or black eyeliner—u know style is about expressing yrself as an individual, not about fitting in. yr look may say "don't bother me" (so don't be surprised if from time 2 time u get kinda lonely), but yr bff's know how much u value their friendship.

if ur a **country girl** at heart, u prolly wear jeans every day (u never know when u might need to ride off into the sunset). but u also can glam it up with high-stepping cowboy boots and bling-worthy earrings. u keep things simple but stylish, knowing just what accessory will catch yr roving cowboy's eye. u set the pace, whether it's doing yr chores out back, organizing a rodeo, or partying with yr bff's, so u'll need to learn when to pull back on the reins a bit.

Send    Cancel

# yr opinion
## swimsuits

**mad maddie:** **swimsuit time. what's yr pref?**
SnowAngel: bikini! bikini! itsy-bitsy, teeny-weeny!
**mad maddie:** **what about my one-piece that makes me look like a bruise? that's good too, tho. right?**
SnowAngel: absolutely not—throw that nasty thing AWAY.
zoegirl: there is no "away," angela. don't u know that?
zoegirl: don't u care about Mother Earth?
SnowAngel: yes, i care very much about Mother Earth . . . and Mother Earth wants maddie to throw it away!!!!!!

|  | yes | no |
|---|---|---|
| speedo (is there *any* guy who can get away with a speedo?) | 🙂 | 🙁 |
| boy shorts | 🙂 | 🙁 |
| board shorts | 🙂 | 🙁 |
| string bikini | 🙂 | 🙁 |
| one-piece | 🙂 | 🙁 |
| tankini | 🙂 | 🙁 |
| skirt | 🙂 | 🙁 |
| peek-a-boo cutouts | 🙂 | 🙁 |

Send  Cancel

# bff

brown as a swimsuit color ........ 👍 👎

black as a swimsuit color ......... 👍 👎

underwire ......................... 👍 👎

thong ............................. 👍 👎

or . . . yr birthday suit ......... 👍 👎

---

**mad maddie:** **oh, kids, all this bathing suit talk is making me want some nestle quik. i find all bathing suits look better with a chocolate milk belly, don't u? and a chocolate milk butt?**

**mad maddie:** **my milkshake brings all the boys to the yard, heh heh heh**

SnowAngel: oh GREAT. this means i have to do extra exercises for u, don't i?

SnowAngel: *and squeeze and lift and squeeze and lift and pump and pump and pump!*

zoegirl: u girls r NUTS.

**mad maddie:** **least we don't *have* nuts. that'd look really weird in a bikini . . .**

SnowAngel: ewwwwwwwwwwwwwwwwwwww! 🍌🍌

Send  Cancel

# another fun thing to do!
## truth or dare?

zoegirl: obviously, this is maddie's game. i was like, "let's have a nice round of scrabble, shall we?"

**mad maddie: and i nixed it. yes, u can thank me l8r, and yes, u can pay me in cookies, preferably very delicious ones of the chocolate chip variety . . .**

SnowAngel: bff's, pick either "truth" or "dare" when it's yr turn. then, the Grand Poo Bah (whoever u choose it to be) gets to pick from the list, and whatever she reads out, u have to do!

zoegirl: but if it involves marshmallows—u get a "get out of jail free" card!!!!

## truth

**mad maddie: tell the truth . . . what is yr worst bad habit?**

_____

_____

zoegirl: what is yr best quality?

_____

_____

SnowAngel: describe yr sexiest pair of undies.

_____

157

SnowAngel: what's the strangest thing u ever did to get yr crush's attention?

**mad maddie: have u ever gone skinny-dipping? wld u ever?**

zoegirl: if u had to spend 3 months on a deserted island, but could bring along 1 guy, who wld it be and why?

SnowAngel: when was the last time someone told u that u were attractive? what did he (or she) say?

**mad maddie: when was the last time someone told u that u were unattractive? what did he (or she) say?**

Send    Cancel

158

zoegirl: confess something that u've been wanting to get off yr chest, but u've been too embarrassed. don't worry. we will hug u. u will feel freer after!!!

SnowAngel: what 3 body parts of yrs r u most satisfied with? what 3 body parts "need improvement"?

**mad maddie: what's the meanest thing u've ever done to anyone?**

zoegirl: what's the nicest thing u've ever done for anyone?

Send   Cancel

**mad maddie:** **u only have 24 hours to live! what do u do?**

zoegirl: if u could have one moment to relive, what wld it be and what wld be different?

SnowAngel: my brilliant bff's, do any of u have other truths u'd like to request?

Send    Cancel

## dare

**mad maddie:** **let's move on to dares. they're more fun.**

**mad maddie:** **how's about ~~march thru yr local mall with marshmallows taped to yr nipples!~~**

zoegirl: nooo! bad girl, maddie! i am CROSSING THAT OUT. try again.

**mad maddie:** **hey, no fair! ur not allowed to cross me out!**

SnowAngel: take a deep breath and try again, mads. u can do it.

**mad maddie:** **~~ok, march thru school with—~~**

zoegirl: NO

**mad maddie:** **seriously—how r u doing that?!!!**

zoegirl: that's for me to know and u to find out. do u think u can suggest an appropriate dare, or do u need to sit in the uncooperative chair?

**mad maddie:** **an "appropriate" dare? sheesh! but fine! march thru yr house—or yr bff's house—with marshmallows taped to yr nipples! can u handle that?!!!**

zoegirl: here's an alternative: stick yr hand in the toilet.

SnowAngel: how about burp yr name?

**mad maddie:** **lick something the group decides on for 5 seconds.**

SnowAngel: attempt to break-dance. (u so fly—or not!)

zoegirl: wear a toilet paper turban.

**mad maddie:** **tuck yr shirt in, then put 5 ice cubes down it. do NOT take them out—let them melt.**

zoegirl: for one minute sing an original and improvised opera.

SnowAngel: show the group a movie kiss—solo.

**mad maddie:** **say the words "in bed" after everything u say for the next 5 minutes.**

| | |
|---|---|
| SnowAngel: | open a window or door and sing the national anthem (loud and proud!) |
| zoegirl: | make a newspaper dress and wear it. |
| **mad maddie:** | **write the name of yr crush on yr hand with indelible ink.** |
| SnowAngel: | lip-synch to any *High School Musical* song. |
| **mad maddie:** | **omg. now THAT wld be torture.** |
| **mad maddie:** | **do any of u have anything else to add?** |

_____

_____

_____

_____

_____

_____

_____

_____

_____

_____

_____

_____

_____

_____

_____

_____

_____

Send    Cancel

# ☺ serious conversation time ☺
## drugs

**mad maddie:** check it out. when i was little, my parents were all, "oh no, little daughter. we *never* did drugs when we were young. never *ever*, little daughter."

**mad maddie:** and then *just last year*, the dads admitted that he and the moms used to be total stoners. can u believe that?!!!

SnowAngel: um . . . we're talking about the mom and dad who raised u, right? the parents who live in yr house and who, like, um, sometimes offer me and zoe beer when we come over? those parents?

**mad maddie:** so what r u saying?

SnowAngel: *shrugs sheepishly while envisioning the Kinnicks toking up*

zoegirl: were *u* surprised, mads? when they told u?

**mad maddie:** no. kinda. surprised they lied for all those years, maybe.

zoegirl: but when u were ten, wld u have wanted to know?

**mad maddie:** i dunno. what shld i tell my kids, if i ever have kids? if they say "what do u think about drugs?" how do i answer?

SnowAngel: what about y'all, bff's? what do y'all think about drugs? hmmmmmmm?

_____

_____

_____

_____

Send      Cancel

# top 5 . . .
## fashion faux pas

zoegirl: isn't it weird how even if u know, rationally, that clothes don't make the man—or in our case, the girl—we still, like, judge ppl by their appearance? even when we try not to?

SnowAngel: yes, it is weird . . . and yes, it's true that we do.

zoegirl: i mean, we can try not to—and i think we shld try not to.

zoegirl: i guess what i'm trying to say is just that there r more important things in life to worry about than if ur wearing the right jeans.

SnowAngel: i'll say . . .

zoegirl: though clothes r fun to talk about—

SnowAngel: i'll say!

**mad maddie: but they r not the end-all-be-all of who we r. got it, chickie.**

SnowAngel: 👍

SnowAngel: *rubs hands together* so, think of those times where u (and u and u, but prolly not me) left the house thinking u looked pretty adorable . . . only to find out l8r that u kinda . . . didn't.

**mad maddie: scrunchies? thong-reveal?**

SnowAngel: partially unwrapped tampon jutting out of cute little clutch? (happened to me at my salon, in front of hot new stylist who, fine, was most likely gay, but u never know, right? it was awful!!!!!)

zoegirl: make a list with yr bff's of y'all's top five fashion faux pas of all times.

164

| | |
|---|---|
| SnowAngel: | feel free to WRITE DOWN FOR ALL OF PERPETUITY the fashion faux pas of—how to say—less beloved girlies, too. |
| SnowAngel: | like tonnie wyndham's rhinestone-studded shirt that spelled T-R-O-U-B-L-E across the chest. one for the books fo sho . . . |

1. _____

2. _____

3. _____

4. _____

5. _____

| | |
|---|---|
| **mad maddie:** | **u know what? i feel better now, after hearing all of y'all's so-embarrassing-u-shld-prolly-never-leave-yr-room-again horror stories! i do!** |
| SnowAngel: | *smiles sunnily and feels suddenly much cuter* |
| SnowAngel: | me too! zo? |
| zoegirl: | um. ok . . . yes! but hopefully u bff's r laffing and feeling better 2. cuz we all do it. |
| **mad maddie:** | **true dat: we all occasionally go out in public looking like crap on a popsicle stick.** |
| SnowAngel: | except me |
| zoegirl: | and if for some reason u rn't feeling better from the simple act of unloading . . . well take comfort in this: yr true-blue 4-evah bff's will luv u no matter what ur wearing. |

# q&a
## all about sibs

| | |
|---|---|
| SnowAngel: | greetings, sissy-poos! |
| zoegirl: | we spend so much time 2gether, we might as well be. |
| SnowAngel: | so, today, i want to talk about real, live sisters . . . or brothers . . . or cousins, if ur an only. |
| zoegirl: | like me, i'm an only. but i can still play. angela says we have to use real live sibs or cousins, but as i am sadly lacking in both, i'm going to use angela and maddie. |
| zoegirl: | so there, angela (and yes, i am sticking my tongue out at u. is that sibling-ish enuff for u?) |
| SnowAngel: | i suppose |
| SnowAngel: | so, siblings . . . |

| | true | false | debatable |
|---|---|---|---|
| r incredibly annoying | ☐ | ☐ | ☐ |
| make the best friends | ☐ | ☐ | ☐ |
| know too much about yr business | ☐ | ☐ | ☐ |
| tell u too much about their business | ☐ | ☐ | ☐ |
| drop yr special facial cleanser brush into the | ☐ | ☐ | ☐ |

Send    Cancel

|  | true | false | debatable |
|---|---|---|---|
| toilet and fail to tell u until *after u've used it* |  |  |  |
| make u feel really good when u give them advice, like when u suggest they set their sights higher than being a supercuts girl when they cld open a salon (one day) of their own | ☐ | ☐ | ☐ |
| defend u no matter what | ☐ | ☐ | ☐ |
| need u to watch out for them every second of the day | ☐ | ☐ | ☐ |
| can do everything better than u can | ☐ | ☐ | ☐ |
| need u to do everything for them | ☐ | ☐ | ☐ |
| won't listen to u | ☐ | ☐ | ☐ |
| always listen to u | ☐ | ☐ | ☐ |

**mad maddie:** u ever tell mark i said this, i will deny it.

**mad maddie:** but i'm glad i can talk to him about things that wld freak out my parents.

Send     Cancel

# bff

| | | true | false | debatable |
|---|---|:---:|:---:|:---:|

zoegirl: that's so sweet! and u know u can always talk 2 us.

SnowAngel: another reason we must have been separated at birth!

zoegirl: what can u talk about with yr sibs?

| | true | false | debatable |
|---|:---:|:---:|:---:|
| boy trouble | ☐ | ☐ | ☐ |
| how to insert a tampon | ☐ | ☐ | ☐ |
| yr latest crush | ☐ | ☐ | ☐ |
| yr bad period cramps | ☐ | ☐ | ☐ |
| whether yr zit is bigger than a house | ☐ | ☐ | ☐ |
| something yr parents said or did that made u mad or hurt yr feelings | ☐ | ☐ | ☐ |
| the fact that u think yr teacher made a pass at u | ☐ | ☐ | ☐ |
| yr problems with yr homework | ☐ | ☐ | ☐ |
| whether u shld try the joint being passed around | ☐ | ☐ | ☐ |

Send    Cancel

|  | true | false | debatable |
|---|---|---|---|
| that ur secretly gay and want to come out | ☐ | ☐ | ☐ |
| what u want to be when u grow up | ☐ | ☐ | ☐ |
| birth control (when u think ur ready to get it) | ☐ | ☐ | ☐ |
| yr personal private family dysfunctions that, sure, every fam has . . . but yrs r more bizarre | ☐ | ☐ | ☐ |
| _____ | ☐ | ☐ | ☐ |
| _____ | ☐ | ☐ | ☐ |

### more q&a

**mad maddie:** **has a sibling ever done that swooping-down superhero thing for u? or have u ever been a supersister 4 yr sibling?**

_____

_____

_____

Send   Cancel

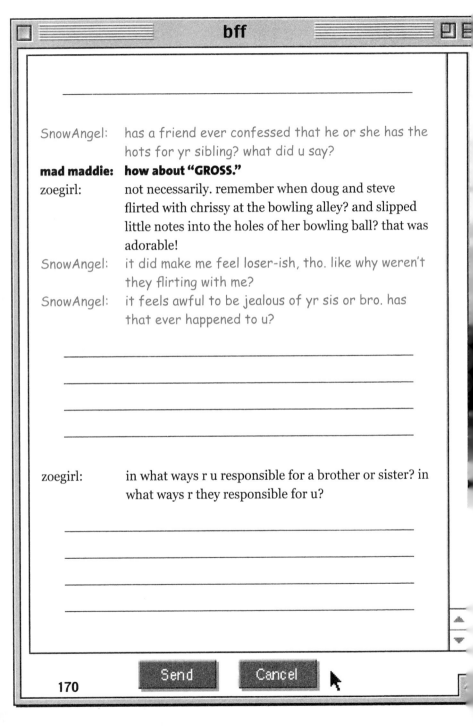

SnowAngel: has a friend ever confessed that he or she has the hots for yr sibling? what did u say?

**mad maddie: how about "GROSS."**

zoegirl: not necessarily. remember when doug and steve flirted with chrissy at the bowling alley? and slipped little notes into the holes of her bowling ball? that was adorable!

SnowAngel: it did make me feel loser-ish, tho. like why weren't they flirting with me?

SnowAngel: it feels awful to be jealous of yr sis or bro. has that ever happened to u?

_____

_____

_____

_____

zoegirl: in what ways r u responsible for a brother or sister? in what ways r they responsible for u?

_____

_____

_____

_____

Send    Cancel

| | |
|---|---|
| SnowAngel: | what's the yuckiest thing yr sibling's ever done? 😦 |
| zoegirl: | like when chrissy dropped yr facial brush in the toilet??? |
| SnowAngel: | while she was using the toilet, mind u! *stomps on picture of chrissy* |

_____

_____

_____

_____

| | |
|---|---|
| zoegirl: | what advice from yr sibs has been really truly absolutely helpful? |

_____

_____

_____

_____

**mad maddie:** **if u could give one bit of advice 2 yr sibs and they wld actually LISTEN what wld it be?**

_____

_____

_____

_____

Send    Cancel

171

| SnowAngel: | and if u could give YRSELF some advice about siblings, what wld it be? *blushes and quickly smooths out picture of chrissy* |
|---|---|

_____

_____

_____

_____

| mad maddie: | **they say ur stuck with yr real family but yr friends r the family u choose** |
|---|---|
| zoegirl: | we *r* family! |
| SnowAngel: | hell yeah! gtg! i'm going shopping with chrissy. |
| mad maddie: | **a family who shops 4 facial brushes together . . .** |
| zoegirl: | stays together! l8r g8r! |

## time out for . . .
# u and yr panis

| zoegirl: | the last one, i gave to angela. here's one for u, mads. |
|---|---|
| SnowAngel: | c? ur getting into it, aren't u? |
| zoegirl: | Plato. I mean, *Virgil*. "Love conquers all . . ." |
| mad maddie: | **ah, yes—with my panis.** |
| mad maddie: | **no wonder i'm so tired . . .** |

Send    Cancel

# another fun thing to do!
## create the soundtrack of yr life, baby!

| | |
|---|---|
| zoegirl: | let's play the soundtrack of yr life. k, how wld u describe yrself? remember—no cheating! the first song pulled randomly from yr iTunes list, that's the one u have to put down! |
| **mad maddie:** | **"nice day for a sulk," belle & sebastian** |
| zoegirl: | hahahaha. perfect! |
| **mad maddie:** | **all right, let's do u. what do u like in a guy?** |
| zoegirl: | fine. what do i like in a guy? |
| zoegirl: | "i kissed a girl" by jill sobule!!! wah!!!! no fair!!!! |
| **mad maddie:** | **oh, zo, i luv u so much. i am rolling here, just so u know!!!!** |
| zoegirl: | do-over, i demand a do-over!!!! |
| **mad maddie:** | **sorry, charlie, no can do** |
| **mad maddie:** | **so fer the rest of u rats, here's what ya do. put yr iTunes on shuffle. For each question, hit "next" under the controls drop-down menu. WRITE DOWN THAT SONG AND DO NOT LIE.** |
| SnowAngel: | then pass the book to the next bff whose turn it is. |
| | |
| zoegirl: | when u were a baby, yr parents described u as: |

_____

_____

_____

_____

| Send | Cancel |
|---|---|

173

SnowAngel: yr best elementary school memory:

_____

_____

_____

_____

zoegirl: if someone says "sum up yr philosophy on life," u say:

_____

_____

_____

_____

**mad maddie: yr worst elementary school memory:**

_____

_____

_____

_____

SnowAngel: yr junior high—past, present, or future—can best be described as:

_____

_____

_____

_____

Send    Cancel

zoegirl:        why u love yr mom:

_____

_____

_____

_____

**mad maddie:**    **the most embarrassing thing that ever happened to u:**

_____

_____

_____

_____

SnowAngel:    if yr friends were talking about u, they'd say:

_____

_____

_____

_____

zoegirl:        when u were little, u thought the happiest thing in the world was:

_____

_____

_____

_____

| Send | Cancel |

SnowAngel:   why u love yr dad:

_____

_____

_____

_____

**mad maddie:   if yr enemies were talking about u, they'd say:**

_____

_____

_____

_____

**mad maddie:   when asked yr opinion on mustaches, u say:**

_____

_____

_____

_____

SnowAngel:   if someone says "hey there, hot stuff!" u say:

_____

_____

_____

_____

Send    Cancel

**mad maddie:    yr excuse for screwing up:**

_____

_____

_____

_____

zoegirl:        when faced with trying to make a hard decision, u:

_____

_____

_____

_____

SnowAngel:    if someone says "pancakes," u say:

_____

_____

_____

_____

zoegirl:        what do u want to be when u grow up?

_____

_____

_____

_____

Send        Cancel

**bff**

**mad maddie:**   **yr bestest ever t-shirt slogan wld be:**

_____

_____

_____

_____

zoegirl:       yr secret fear is:

_____

_____

_____

_____

SnowAngel:   u love yr friends so much that sometimes u say to
them:

_____

_____

_____

_____

**mad maddie:**   **when ur sad, u:**

_____

_____

_____

_____

Send        Cancel

178

# lauren myracle

zoegirl:        when ur filled with joy, u:

_____

_____

_____

_____

SnowAngel:   if u cld lead someone else's life, u'd choose:

_____

_____

_____

zoegirl:        when u reach the end of yr life's journey, u'll say:

_____

_____

_____

**mad maddie:   what will they play at yr funeral? (not to be morbid . . .)**

_____

_____

_____

_____

Send   Cancel

**SnowAngel:** and now it is the final scene of the movie of yr life, which u have so brilliantly created this soundtrack for. as u ascend to heaven, if there is a heaven to ascend to, what song will be playing? (and just this once u don't have to let iTunes choose. u yrself can choose the most perfect Ascension song ever!!!)

_____

_____

_____

_____

Send    Cancel

## ☺ serious conversation time ☺
### stealing

SnowAngel:   bff's: have any of y'all ever stolen anything before?

**mad maddie:** **why r u asking them THAT?**

SnowAngel:   *shrugs* just curious. and plus sometimes it's good to, ya know, get stuff off yr chest. IF u have anything to get off yr chest.

**mad maddie:** **well, i want to add a twist to it. I'm thinking of peeps like zoe, who i'm fairly certain hasn't stolen anything, ever. zo? am i right?**

zoegirl:   i've never stolen anything, no. i wld feel so guilty. like, forever.

zoegirl:   but wait—does almost stealing something count? i *almost* stole boo boo bear from jana when jana was being so awful to y'all! remember?

**mad maddie:** **which brings me to my question, to be answered along with angela's question. is there any situation where stealing wld be the right thing to do, even if it was still—obviously—"wrong"?**

_____

_____

_____

_____

_____

_____

_____

Send    Cancel

181

# yr opinion
## tattoos

**mad maddie:** tat time! i am gonna get me some tats before too long.
SnowAngel: tats, plural?
**mad maddie:** yup. But instead of saying MOTHER in curlicue script, mine'll be a heart, and in it it'll say THE WINSOME THREESOME.
SnowAngel: in curlicue font
**mad maddie:** of course! maybe a rose thrown in, maybe a 'stache . . .
SnowAngel: a rose with a 'stache! YES!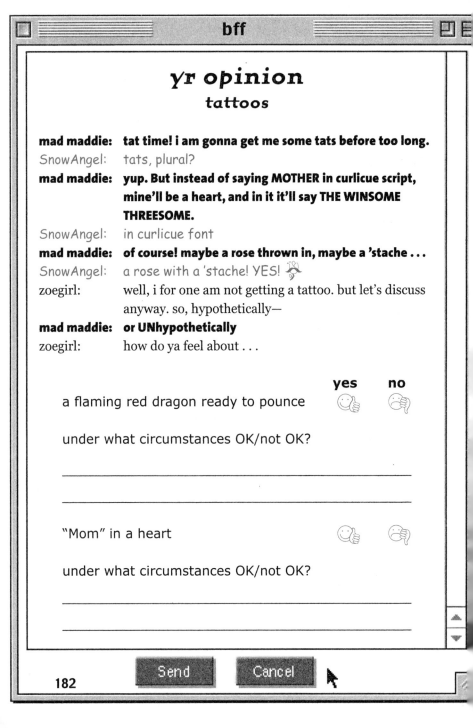
zoegirl: well, i for one am not getting a tattoo. but let's discuss anyway. so, hypothetically—
**mad maddie:** or UNhypothetically
zoegirl: how do ya feel about . . .

|  | yes | no |
|---|---|---|
| a flaming red dragon ready to pounce |  |  |

under what circumstances OK/not OK?

_____

_____

"Mom" in a heart

under what circumstances OK/not OK?

_____

_____

Send     Cancel

182

the name of a boyfriend or girlfriend

under what circumstances OK/not OK?

_____

_____

2 cute little cherries, connected at
the stem

under what circumstances OK/not OK?

_____

_____

Mickey Mouse

under what circumstances OK/not OK?

_____

_____

a tattoo on yr shoulder

under what circumstances OK/not OK?

_____

_____

Send    Cancel

**bff**

a tattoo on yr chest

under what circumstances OK/not OK?

_____

_____

a tattoo on yr neck

under what circumstances OK/not OK?

_____

_____

a tattoo on yr butt that says "i ♡ maddie"

under what circumstances OK/not OK?

_____

_____

a full-body tattoo

under what circumstances OK/not OK?
and what wld it be of????

_____

_____

_____

Send    Cancel

184

# yr opinion
## piercings

| | |
|---|---|
| **mad maddie:** | **so—which one of us is gonna get her nipples pierced first, eh?** |
| SnowAngel: | *pales* |
| SnowAngel: | NOT me |
| zoegirl: | not me! |
| **mad maddie:** | **labia?** |
| SnowAngel: | she's not here right now, sorry. |
| SnowAngel: | (that was a joke, btw. tee-hee. like u were going around the room asking who was gonna be first, and angela (that's me) said no, and then zo, and so u were like, "Melanie? Holly? Labia?") |
| **mad maddie:** | **oh, angela, there's nothing like a good joke, is there?** |
| zoegirl: | and that was NOTHING like a good joke! |
| **mad maddie:** | **ba dum DUM** |
| SnowAngel: | *rolls eyes* |
| SnowAngel: | oh u silly silly gulls . . . |
| SnowAngel: | so what IS ok to pierce? and of course u can specify whether ur saying ok for u, ok for yr bff, ok for a guy, whatever. . . |

                                                            **yes**      **no**

top of ear

under what circumstances OK/not OK?

_____

_____

Send    Cancel

# bff

earlobe 🙂👍 🙁👎

under what circumstances OK/not OK?

_____

_____

multiple ear piercings 🙂👍 🙁👎

under what circumstances OK/not OK?

_____

_____

nostril 🙂👍 🙁👎

under what circumstances OK/not OK?

_____

_____

nasal septum (u know, that bit 🙂👍 🙁👎
of flesh between yr nostrils?)
under what circumstances OK/not OK?

_____

_____

tongue 🙂👍 🙁👎

Send   Cancel

under what circumstances OK/not OK?

_____

_____

nipple

under what circumstances OK/not OK?

_____

_____

eyebrow

under what circumstances OK/not OK?

_____

_____

ear "stretchers"

zoegirl:     i think they're gross, btw. i don't get the point.

under what circumstances OK/not OK?

_____

_____

ear "dumbbells"

Send     Cancel

under what circumstances OK/not OK?

_____

_____

belly button    🙂👍    🙁👎

under what circumstances OK/not OK?

_____

_____

labia    🙂👍    🙁👎

**mad maddie:**    **hahaha! u knew we'd get to that one eventually!!!!**
**mad maddie:**    **save the best for last, hmm? *hmmm?!***

under what circumstances OK/not OK?

_____

_____

Send    Cancel

## top 5 things
### that u love OR HATE about
### vampires . . . to discuss . . . or not

**mad maddie:** **i vote "not." vampires r so yesterday. they r dead to me, baby.**

**mad maddie:** **(heh heh heh—now THAT was a joke, a.)**

zoegirl: we could compare them to werewolves, i guess. do y'all want to have that debate?

SnowAngel: i'd rather do unicorns versus zombies.

zoegirl: but it says *vampires* at the top of the page.

SnowAngel: i know, let's do that thing where the teacher says, "plz answer this question," and we say, "okay!" only in reality we answer whatever question we want to, and the teacher doesn't notice cuz we do such a sneaky lead in!

zoegirl: totally! like, we cld pretend we're on a talk show, and Tyra—

SnowAngel: *strikes vogue pose* or me. i cld be the talk show host!

zoegirl: ok, so i'm yr guest on The Angela Hour—

**mad maddie:** **exsqueeze me, isn't that an oxymoron? isn't every hour angela hour?**

zoegirl: hmm. true, but not sure "oxymoron" is the right term . . .

zoegirl: what's the word for when something is completely self-evident? so self-evident that to say it is like totally—REDUNDANT! yes!

**mad maddie:** **welcome to The Redundant Angela Hour! and today our special guest is sexpert Dr. Zoe Barrett, who knows all**

|  |  |
|---|---|
|  | **there is to know about communing with the undead.** |
|  | **Dr. Z, let's discuss vampires. love 'em or hate 'em?** |
| zoegirl: | riiiight, not where i was heading but i'll work with it. |
| zoegirl: | so AFTER clarifying that i am not a "sex"pert in *any*thing— |
| SnowAngel: | yeah, mads. u don't bring a sexpert in to discuss the undead. then it's like hydrophilia. |
| zoegirl: | uh, no, hydrophilia is love of water. i think u mean hemophilia, which is love of blood? |
| mad maddie: | **actually, i think she means necrophilia: love of DEAD PPL.** |
| mad maddie: | **but zo, i'm pretty impressed with yr knowledge of "philias."** |
| zoegirl: | oh, i am all about the philia. i have a whole book of them. like, i am a bibliophile: i love books. angela, ur a laliophile, which means u love talking, and mads, ur an eleutherophile. that means u love freedom. |
| mad maddie: | **why, yes. yes i do. thumbs-up.** |
| zoegirl: | then there's apotemnophilia, which is love of ppl with amputations. or if u want an even stranger one, there's defecaloesiophilia: the love of painful bowel movements. |
| zoegirl: | i wldn't ordinarily throw that one out there, btw, except i know mads will love it. |
| mad maddie: | **do i EVER. u have just provided me with my newest insult, z-boogie!!! course i'll have to learn how to pronounce it . . . so that it slips easily off my tongue . . .** |
| mad maddie: | **as opposed to a "bowel movement" which does NOT slip easily from—** |
| SnowAngel: | *zips maddie's lips* ok, all done! thanks for playing! |
| SnowAngel: | zo, r we ever finishing the deft vampires-to-unicorns switcheroo? |

Send    Cancel

# lauren myracle

| | |
|---|---|
| zoegirl: | YES! so i'm on the talk show, and angela asks how i feel about vampires, and i say, "ah, yes, vampires. did u know that in ancient Nordic mythology, unicorns predated vampires by 2000 years? and speaking of unicorns . . ." |
| zoegirl: | c how easy? |
| SnowAngel: | vair vair clever, u! is that true, whatever u just said? |
| zoegirl: | of course not, but that doesn't matter. |
| **mad maddie:** | **on with the discussion, then. top 5 things you love and hate about vampires or werewolves or unicorns or zombies. go!** |

love:

1. _____
2. _____
3. _____
4. _____
5. _____

hate:

1. _____
2. _____
3. _____
4. _____
5. _____

Send    Cancel

191

# quiz

SnowAngel:   yay, quizzes! *dances about spazzerifically*

zoegirl:   r u a vampire?

**mad maddie:   or a werewolf?**

SnowAngel:   or a cute li'l cuddly unicorn?

**mad maddie:   or a ZOMBIE?**

zoegirl:   the truth shall set u free!

|   |   | true | false |
|---|---|:---:|:---:|
| 1. | everybody loves u—except stupid unicorn-haters, and who needs them, anyway? 🦄 | ☐ | ☐ |
| 2. | u like to sleep during the day. | ☐ | ☐ |
| 3. | u tend to go out at night. | ☐ | ☐ |
| 4. | yr boyfriend likes to watch u sleep . . . and one day u want to be just like him. | ☐ | ☐ |
| 5. | yr complexion is super pale. | ☐ | ☐ |
| 6. | ur highly sensitive to sunlight or other bright light. | ☐ | ☐ |
| 7. | u lurch. | ☐ | ☐ |

bff

Send    Cancel

192

|  |  | true | false |
|---|---|:---:|:---:|
| 8. | black becomes u. | ☐ | ☐ |
| 9. | u single-paw-edly keep Tweez-erman, manufacturer of heavy-duty tweezers, in business. | ☐ | ☐ |
| 10. | u hate garlic. | ☐ | ☐ |
| 11. | u love flowers. and frolicking. | ☐ | ☐ |
| 12. | people find u interesting . . . at first. then a little creepy. | ☐ | ☐ |
| 13. | u feel misplaced in the 21st century. | ☐ | ☐ |
| 14. | u have a bad odor of rotting-flesh . . . yr own. | ☐ | ☐ |
| 15. | ur always, *always* ripping yr clothes at the seams. | ☐ | ☐ |
| 16. | u go as yrself on Halloween. | ☐ | ☐ |
| 17. | u have a unibrow. | ☐ | ☐ |
| 18. | u have yet to find a hat that becomes u. | ☐ | ☐ |

Send    Cancel    ▶

|  | true | false |
|---|---|---|
| 19. ur able to shape-shift. | ☐ | ☐ |
| 20. u don't cast a shadow. | ☐ | ☐ |
| 21. u find yrself chasing delivery trucks, barking. | ☐ | ☐ |
| 22. full moons drive u ker-azy! | ☐ | ☐ |
| 23. u avoid mirrors—they don't reflect the true u. | ☐ | ☐ |
| 24. u like to drink blood. | ☐ | ☐ |
| 25. if someone drove a stake through yr heart, u'd die. | ☐ | ☐ |

**mad maddie: duh.**

# quiz results!

**mad maddie: ah, u don't need help scoring this one, do ya?**

zoegirl:     u know who u r—and guess what? we love u anyway!

SnowAngel:   unless ur a creepy ZOMBIE, in which case we wld like u to leave now, plz.

SnowAngel:   or rehabilitate yrself . . .

Send     Cancel

# yr bff flicklist
## crazy scary

SnowAngel:   sometimes it's fun to get scared . . .

**mad maddie:** **as long as ur not TRULY being pursued by slobbering, lurching zombies who want nothing more than to rip yr limbs off like toothpicks.**

zoegirl:   but i don't like slasher movies. they creep me out and get in my head, and then i'm stuck with those images when i least want them.

zoegirl:   i like psychological thrillers, tho . . .

SnowAngel:   make yr group list of scariest, most bone-chilly-ing flicks evah—and sure, since u all have yr different takes on things, it's cool if some r slashers, some r classics, some r psychological thrillers.

**mad maddie:** **and then just talk about 'em and shit. ooo, maybe even rent one . . .**

_____

_____

_____

_____

_____

_____

_____

_____

Send    Cancel

195

# yr bff playlist
## nitey-nite

| | |
|---|---|
| SnowAngel: | eeek, i'm all shivery now. zoe, ur right! i don't want these images in my brain! |
| **mad maddie:** | **too bad, so sad. alas.** |
| zoegirl: | not true—and wow, mads. i'm so impressed with yr sensitivity. |
| **mad maddie:** | **heh heh heh, i'm just kidding my girl** |
| SnowAngel: | zoe, u said "not true." u have a trick to de-shiverize myself? especially tonite, when bedtime rolls around, and i'm alone in my dark dark room???? |
| zoegirl: | WELL. y'all know i have sleep issues anyway, right? |
| **mad maddie:** | **cuz ur type a and strung-out. go on.** |
| zoegirl: | so i made myself a "nitey-nite" playlist that is calm and soothing and beautiful, and then i play it when i go to sleep. |
| SnowAngel: | oh |
| SnowAngel: | on yr iPod? doesn't that, like, run the battery down? |
| **mad maddie:** | **all iPods have "sleep" functions, a. hunt around for it; u'll find it.** |
| SnowAngel: | all right, cool. then let's make a nitey-nite playlist right now! everyone write down a most excellent slow-down-and-chill song, then pass the list around . . . and around . . . and—*takes break to yawn*—hey! it's working already! |

Send    Cancel

Send  Cancel

# another fun thing to do!
## plan a road trip, baby!!!

**mad maddie:** **so what if it's fantasy land. plan it anywayz!**

SnowAngel: crank up the music, roll down the windows, and just GO. 😎

zoegirl: omigosh, that wld be \*so\* cool!!!

**mad maddie:** **what's yr destination?**

---

SnowAngel: who r yr travel buds?

---

---

---

zoegirl: what kind of car will u drive?

---

zoegirl: and u'll need to plan what u'll bring a few days ahead of time. make a packing list here.

---

---

---

---

---

Send     Cancel

_____

_____

_____

_____

_____

_____

**mad maddie:** whatever u do, don't forget munchies for the car. let's
list those here, too.

_____

_____

_____

_____

_____

### time out for . . .
### u and yr panis

**mad maddie:** here's one from Alfred Hitchcock. i don't know how
inspirational it is, but it makes me laff.

**mad maddie:** "In films, murders are always very clean. I show how
difficult it is and what a messy thing is it to kill a man . . ."

SnowAngel: with my panis! tee-hee!

Send    Cancel

# yr bff playlist
## on the road

SnowAngel:    *grows amazing Willie Nelson braids and dons black leather vest* "on the road again! i just can't wait to get on the road again!"

SnowAngel:    mmm, mmm, mmm, that is a good song.

**mad maddie:  willie nelson's da man. not that i actually have any of his songs on my iPod, but i suppose that cld change 1 day.**

**mad maddie:  did either of y'all c stephen colbert's Christmas special that 1 year? when willie was one of three wise men, only miniaturized so that he fit into stephen colbert's manger scene? and he sings about the plant that, um, smokes more sweetly than either frankincense or myrrh?**

**mad maddie:  it is GENIUS**

SnowAngel:    *looks stern*

SnowAngel:    i thought yr stoner days were OVER, mads!

**mad maddie:  doesn't mean I can't appreciate good humor! And really: how else is it possible that the shepherds and the wise men thought a star was talking to them, huh? i ask u!**

zoegirl:      moving on. start yr list with "on the road again" if u want, and then do the thing where u pass it from bff to bff, until u have the most excellent road trip playlist ever.

**mad maddie:  "drive" by incubus comes to mind—oh, and "shut up and drive" by rihanna**

SnowAngel:    maybe that oldie-but-goodie, "girls just wanna have fun"?

200

zoegirl:       or—i know! let's let them decide, our new bff buds!
              novel concept, i know . . .

Send      Cancel

# yr bff playlist
## overplayed ditties that still rock yr socks off

| | |
|---|---|
| zoegirl: | c, this is so cool. with all these playlists, we're gonna have a HUGE collection of awesome . . . um . . . collections! |
| SnowAngel: | and they will always remind us of US, and we will look at each other and go, awwwww! |
| **mad maddie:** | **so make this list be all those awesome songs that, sure, maybe r overdone. but who cares? u still like 'em, right?** |
| SnowAngel: | if u don't, don't put 'em down . . . |
| zoegirl: | don't forget "hey there, Delilah" by plain white T's |
| SnowAngel: | or "year 3000" by the jonas brothers—and maddie, shut up. IT IS A GOOD SONG. |
| SnowAngel: | ooo, and "barbie girl" by aqua!!!! |
| SnowAngel: | *flips hair and smiles plastically* i'm a Barbie girl, in a Barbie wor-r-rld! life in plastic, it's fanTASti-ic! |
| zoegirl: | and also I think u shld include the theme song to *beverly hills cop*. "Axel F," I think it's called? |
| **mad maddie:** | **r u writing tiny in the hopes of avoiding my scorn?** |
| zoegirl: | maybe |
| **mad maddie:** | **well I think u shld follow yr own advice and let the bff's write their own frickin' list!!!! (just as long as they include "disturbia," of course.)** |

_____

_____

_____

_____

Send    Cancel

Send    Cancel

# another fun thing to do!
## make the movie of yr life (so far)!

SnowAngel: now, while we all know that johnny depp cld play any one of us and make it work, i for one wld rather go with . . . hmm, that cute actress from shopaholic. amy adams?

zoegirl: nope, u mean Isla Fisher

SnowAngel: i do? huh.

**mad maddie: there r other deets to consider—in this fine movie of yr life that will no doubt be picked up by Disney—than just who's gonna play u.**

SnowAngel: mads? yrs will NOT be a Disney movie.

**mad maddie: er . . . true. but zoe's cld be! she cld even get that demi lovato chick to play her!**

SnowAngel: maddie's right, tho. there r other things to consider. how about u? before the cameras start rolling, u need 2 answer a few questions.

zoegirl: is yr life a . . .

    a. Hollywood blockbuster
    b. or a cool indie flick?

SnowAngel: and is yr story a . . .

    a. romance
    b. comedy
    c. romantic comedy
    d. tragedy
    e. suspense

Send    Cancel

    f.  swashbuckling adventure
    g.  science fiction
    h.  fantasy
    i.  true-to-life
    j.  _____

**mad maddie:   what's the title going to be?**

_____

zoegirl:      and who will play u and why?

_____

SnowAngel:   super important!!!!!! who will play yr LOVE
             INTEREST?

_____

**mad maddie:   and each of yr bff's. don't forget them!**

_____
_____
_____

zoegirl:      do u wanna include yr parents or siblings?

_____
_____
_____

Send      Cancel

SnowAngel: and is there other supporting cast?

**mad maddie: and, ooooo, scary music is playing . . . the evil force is . . .**

zoegirl: remember, tho, it's yr movie and u don't have to invite him or her to participate if u don't want 2.

SnowAngel: add a soundtrack!

SnowAngel: now let yr buds check out yr choices and give THEIR opinions.

SnowAngel: and then start preparing yr Oscar speech for best director! and best screenplay! and best female lead, cuz even if isla is in it, she doesn't get to accept the award!

Send    Cancel

# promises to yr adult self

**mad maddie:** **dudes, we're gonna get old one day. WE—yes, us—will be old-heads.**

SnowAngel: eee-gads, way to bring the party down

SnowAngel: *makes sad whine and whizzes about room like a deflating balloon (which nonetheless is a pink balloon, even if it is all wrinkly)*

zoegirl: I don't think that's the right attitude AT ALL. we're gonna grow up . . . so? what wld u rather have happen? wld u rather die young?

SnowAngel: *whizzes and whines even more frenetically*

SnowAngel: now that's a lovely thought, zo! sheesh!

zoegirl: i think the key is to just not become *depressing* grown-ups.

**mad maddie:** **to not rot, u mean**

zoegirl: uh . . . I guess

SnowAngel: ewww

**mad maddie:** **then let's make it happen. NO ROTTING OLD-HEADS. Let's make some promises here and now about our future selves, k?**

i will never wear _____

_____

i will never say _____

_____

Send    Cancel

i will never make my kids eat _____

_____

i will never freak out about _____

_____

I will never yell at my kids about _____

_____

while wearing my Spanx "Shaping Bodysuit" and

nothing else, i will never _____

_____

i will never listen to _____

_____

i will never dye my hair _____

_____

i will never live in _____

_____

i will never waste time doing _____

_____

Send    Cancel

i will never lose touch with _____

_____

i will never forget how it feels to _____

_____

i will never . . . _____

_____

_____

_____

_____

_____

_____

_____

i will always love to _____

_____

i will always wear my _____

_____

i will always listen to _____

Send    Cancel

_____

i will always play _____

_____

i will always keep _____

_____

i will always be _____

_____

i will always tell my kids _____

_____

i will always be adventuresome when it comes to _____

_____

whenever i ever feel sad and don't know why, i will
always pick up my phone and call _____

_____

I will always save time for _____

_____

Send    Cancel

# lauren myracle ▭ 目

I will always be grateful for _____

_____

I will always remember _____

_____

I will always . . . _____

_____

_____

_____

_____

_____

_____

_____

_____

_____

_____

_____

_____

_____

| Send | Cancel |

211

# ☺ **serious conversation time** ☺
## faith

| | |
|---|---|
| zoegirl: | ppl get weirded out talking about God. have y'all noticed that? |
| **mad maddie:** | **well, maybe some ppl prefer not to talk about God. is that a problem?** |
| zoegirl: | noooooo . . . but why is that? |
| zoegirl: | do *u* prefer not to talk about God, maddie? |
| **mad maddie:** | **if i'm around ppl i feel judged by . . .** |
| zoegirl: | do u feel judged by me? |
| SnowAngel: | of course she doesn't. |
| SnowAngel: | do u? |
| **mad maddie:** | **grrrrrr** |
| **mad maddie:** | **no, not really. but i dunno, the whole subject does make me feel a little uncomfortable.** |
| zoegirl: | and c, that's so fascinating, cuz i love talking about God and faith and stuff like that. like, does God even exist? |
| **mad maddie:** | **and what about the Great Cheese Puff in the sky? shld we be bowing at the feet of the Great Cheese Puff in the sky?** |
| zoegirl: | maddie, cheese puffs don't have feet |
| SnowAngel: | bff's—what do y'all think? ✝ ✡ ☯ ☪ ☽ |

Send     Cancel

# yr bff playlist
## mellow yellow

SnowAngel: \*sits in lotus position with hands held palm up\*
SnowAngel: ommmmm. ommmmmm.
zoegirl: u know what i do when i need to listen to mellow songs? I go to Pandora radio and listen to the Bon Iver station i made. and then if i discover a new song I LOVE, i go to iTunes and buy it.
**mad maddie: music does help me chill, for sure. sometimes u wanna get hyped up, sometimes u wanna be calmed down ...**
**mad maddie: make a list of chillaxers, k? u know the drill ... pass the list around ... everybody add her fave ... be zen ...**
SnowAngel: \*makes peace fingers\* peace out, bff's!

_____
_____
_____
_____
_____
_____
_____
_____
_____
_____
_____

Send    Cancel

## q&a
### life happens

SnowAngel: hello, bff's. *looks around furtively*
SnowAngel: perhaps ur wondering why i've gathered u here today. *looks around furtively again*
SnowAngel: well . . . it's to talk about. . . well . . . inspirational quotes! which i love!!!! but maddie wld roll her eyes and zoe might possibly do the same thing, only more politely, cuz my quotes-to-live-by rn't always, ya know, deep enuff for her.
SnowAngel: so let's keep this just b/w us, shall we?
SnowAngel: great! ☺
SnowAngel: SO. what quote best sums up yr philosophy on life?

___ "Every thought is a possibility." —Indigo Girls, "Mystery"

___ "I am not afraid of storms for I am learning how to sail my ship." —Louisa May Alcott

___ "Life is what happens when you're busy making other plans." —John Lennon, "Beautiful Boy"

___ "Fill your life with love and bravery, and you shall live a life uncommon." —Jewel, "Life Uncommon"

___ "You have brains in your head. You have feet in your shoes. You can steer yourself in any direction you choose. You're on your own. And you know what you

Send    Cancel

know. You are the guy who'll decide where to go."
—Dr. Seuss, *Oh, The Places You'll Go!*

\_\_ "Fashions fade—style is eternal." —Yves Saint Laurent

\_\_ "It matters not what someone is born, but what they
grow to be." —J. K. Rowling, *Harry Potter and the
Goblet of Fire*

\_\_ "My philosophy is that not only are you responsible
for your life, but doing the best at this moment puts
you in the best place for the next moment."
—Oprah Winfrey

SnowAngel:   do u, like, have yr OWN quote? if so, write it down.
if not—yep! write it down anyway! which means first
figuring it out . . .

Send     Cancel

# ☺ **serious conversation time** ☺
## *afterlife*

zoegirl: i want to talk about religion more. can we talk about religion more?

SnowAngel: sure, i'm game

zoegirl: well, what do u think happens after ppl die? do u believe in souls? do u believe in life after death?

SnowAngel: *blinks*

SnowAngel: um, ur not truly asking ME, are u? cuz i sure don't know!

zoegirl: i don't either, not for sure. but i like wondering.

zoegirl: bff's—what do y'all believe?

Send    Cancel

# yr bff flicklist
## all time favorites EVAH

SnowAngel:    we've talked about horror movies . . .
**mad maddie:**   **sappy movies . . .**
zoegirl:       "girl time" movies and "boyfriend" movies.
SnowAngel:    now list yr fave flicks of all time. leave no fave flick
                   unnamed!!!!

Send      Cancel

# things to do before u graduate
# . . . or get married . . . or die

SnowAngel:   like our own bucket list, right? things to do before
             we kick the bucket?

**mad maddie:   exactly, but u can tailor 'em to a specific point in yr life
             if u want.**

zoegirl:     like, if u wanna go skinny-dipping, maybe "before i
             graduate from college" is better than "before i am too
             weak to leave my bed at the old folks' home."

**mad maddie:   then again . . . old folks can go skinny-dipping. no law
             against it!**

SnowAngel:   U want to go skinny-dipping, zoe barrett?

**mad maddie:   while wearing Depends?!!**

zoegirl:     oh-ho, but that wouldn't be skinny-dipping, now wld it?

SnowAngel:   *licks finger and sizzles it against fanny*

SnowAngel:   she got u, mads! hahahahaha!


before I graduate I will:

\_\_\_ kiss the boy I really like

\_\_\_ defend the person in my grade who everyone else
     picks on

\_\_\_ eat alone in a sit-down restaurant without feeling
     like a loser

\_\_\_ have a nighttime picnic with my bff's

218

____ drive without having someone in the front passenger's seat slam on a pretend brake pedal

____ tell someone I admire how I feel without blushing as red as a tomato

____ make an appointment with a gynecologist . . . and *go!*

____ laugh so hard while drinking milk that it comes out of my nose

____ tell off my worst enemy, without losing my cool

____ go snorkeling or skydiving or hang gliding or rappelling

____ volunteer for a cause or organization that I believe in

____ strike up a conversation with my crush (it can even be about something lame like the weather or frappuccino flavors)

____ design and sew a piece of clothing for myself

____ write a poem, story, essay, or song

____ try out for a part in a school production. if i'm really feeling hyped, try out for the lead!

____ learn a new sport or try out for a team

Send    Cancel

\_\_\_ make a YouTube video

\_\_\_ perform a routine in the school talent show

\_\_\_ start a blog

\_\_\_ get a makeover

\_\_\_ travel somewhere by myself

\_\_\_ _____

\_\_\_ _____

\_\_\_ _____

\_\_\_ _____

before I get married i will . . .

\_\_\_ launch my own company

\_\_\_ play or sing in a band

\_\_\_ get a beehive hairdo . . . just once for fun!

\_\_\_ take up surfing

\_\_\_ learn to knit

\_\_\_ have my own apartment

Send    Cancel

# lauren myracle

\_\_\_ live in a foreign country

\_\_\_ appear on *American Idol*

\_\_\_ learn how to fly a plane

\_\_\_ speak another language fluently

\_\_\_ change my style dramatically

\_\_\_ stop a bad habit (like nail biting, hair twirling, or temper tantrums)

\_\_\_ not obsess about how I look the day after I get my hair cut

\_\_\_ not freak out or sulk when someone makes me angry

\_\_\_ count the rings of a tree

\_\_\_ watch the sun dip beneath the horizon

\_\_\_ go on a road trip across the country with my bff's

\_\_\_ go skinny-dipping in winter

\_\_\_ ride a camel or an elephant

\_\_\_ see every *Twilight Zone* episode

Send   Cancel

___ learn to cook an entire meal, from appetizers to desserts, and make it for a special someone

___ spend the night in an igloo

___ chew one piece of gum from dawn until midnight

___ meet an honest-to-goodness hero—or be one!

___ give up my favorite but totally unhealthy snack food

___ own a horse

___ _____

___ _____

___ _____

___ _____

before I die, I will . . .

___ find true love

___ have kids of my own

___ walk on Mars

___ be a great cook

Send    Cancel

\_\_\_\_ buy an haute-couture gown and have somewhere to wear it

\_\_\_\_ run for president

\_\_\_\_ ride in a hot-air balloon

\_\_\_\_ write a novel

\_\_\_\_ travel around the world

\_\_\_\_ climb a very high mountain

\_\_\_\_ sail across the ocean

\_\_\_\_ learn sign language

\_\_\_\_ get really good at something

\_\_\_\_ be able to say I love what I do

\_\_\_\_ do something to make the world a better place

\_\_\_\_ _____

\_\_\_\_ _____

\_\_\_\_ _____

\_\_\_\_ _____

# ☺ **serious conversation time** ☺
## *flaws*

SnowAngel:     i for one think we have had some pretty darn
                 \*serious\* "serious conversations" lately. so for this
                 one, i hereby give y'all permission to be serious OR
                 silly.

**mad maddie:**    **or both!**

SnowAngel:     if u cld change ONE THING about yrself, what wld
                 it be?

zoegirl:       and why????

_____

_____

_____

_____

_____

_____

_____

_____

_____

_____

_____

Send      Cancel

## ? ? q&a ? ?
### ? predict the future ?

SnowAngel: time to pretend we r 10 again, and on a car trip,
a l-o-n-g car trip, and we're all squished in the
backseat, and zoe is stuck in the middle. k?

zoegirl: why am i stuck in the middle?

**mad maddie: cuz ur the smallest—and no going over my line!!!!**

SnowAngel: tee-hee. and we r bored, and we have already named
our pretend children, and we have NOT used names
like "Amber Sue" or "Nurylon."

**mad maddie: hey, speak for yrself!**

SnowAngel: so now it is time . . . ta-DA! to look into our magic
crystal balls and predict our futures!!!!

**mad maddie: let's start with the not-so-distant future, just to get
warmed up:**

**mad maddie: what will u be doing a year from now:**

_____

_____

_____

_____

SnowAngel: what will be yr least favorite phys ed fitness
test?

_____

_____

Send    Cancel

zoegirl:        which shoes will be yr favorites?

SnowAngel:      who will be yr best buds?

**mad maddie:   duh. the ones u have now, dummy.**

SnowAngel:      what about yr love life? 😊 who r u going to be
                dating? does he treat u like the princess u r? tell
                me everything about him.

zoegirl:        what will u have to write about when u apply to the
                college of yr choice? what activities will u have? a job
                after school or on weekends? what clubs will u b in?

Send    Cancel

**mad maddie:** don't get stuck in the same old same old. pick one thing that will be totally different about u. something cool like u can pitch a perfect game and not that u have braces (unless they r off and u have straight pearly whites at last).

zoegirl: where u go to college is super important and i don't mean where yr prnts want u to go to college!!!!

SnowAngel: u could stay in yr hometown 4 college or u could go far, far away, never to be seen again (like a certain other person i know)?

zoegirl: angela! maddie is never far away in spirit.

**mad maddie: right on**

zoegirl: anyway, where will u go to college? in what state or country? what will u study?

**mad maddie:** so where will u be in 5 years?

**mad maddie:** where will u b living? what will yr major be? what amazible things will u have seen? do u have a serious boyfriend? do u live together?

———————————————

———————————————

———————————————

———————————————

SnowAngel: in 10 years u'll be like a real adult! who will u be dating and what will he be like? or OMG! r u married??? tell me, who is the lucky guy? do u—*gulps*—have kids?!!!!

———————————————

———————————————

———————————————

———————————————

zoegirl: i hope hope hope u've landed yr dream job. what is it? tell us everything!

———————————————

———————————————

———————————————

———————————————

Send    Cancel

| | |
|---|---|
| **mad maddie:** | **ok, here's a stretch . . . where will u b in 25 years?** |
| zoegirl: | what is yr life like? yr career, yr house, what do u look like? how often do u see yr bff's from high school? |
| **mad maddie:** | **what amazing things have u done? god forbid ur acting like an old-head.** |

_____

_____

_____

_____

| | |
|---|---|
| SnowAngel: | i'll always know my bff's! hey, what about in 50 years? |
| zoegirl: | omg. we'll be sweet old ladies who get together to discuss our grandchildren! will we even have grandchildren? will we still love our husbands? |
| **mad maddie:** | **will we play bingo and drink pink wine? hey, maybe we'll be three old battle axes!** |
| SnowAngel: | as long as we're still friends, that's what counts. |
| SnowAngel: | but seriously, where do u think u'll be and what will u be doing? |

_____

_____

_____

_____

Send    Cancel

# yr bff playlist
## underappreciated gems

| | |
|---|---|
| zoegirl: | angela? u may not put "come clean" by hilary duff on this list. |
| SnowAngel: | oh yes i can—just watch me. it is a GREAT song and reminds me of good times (ahhhh, *Cinderella Story*), so just hush. |
| SnowAngel: | but u! u my little nutcase! i absolutely forbid u from putting on that perky-as-heck song u learned at friday morning fellowship. |
| SnowAngel: | how did that song go? |
| zoegirl: | "think about think about think about GOD! if u don't think about nothin' else!" |
| zoegirl: | it's such a *happy* song! |
| **mad maddie:** | **it's definitely underappreciated. in fact it's full-out unappreciated, at least by me and my 5000 closest friends.** |
| zoegirl: | well, don't worry. i do get a kick out of that song, but it doesn't make the cut for the official "underappreciated" playlist. for my first song, when the list comes to me, I think i'll put . . . "i'll be yr bird" by m. ward. |
| SnowAngel: | ??? |
| SnowAngel: | me not know that song |
| zoegirl: | hence, "underappreciated." check it out. it's fab. (it cld be a double-hitter for our mellow yellow playlist, too . . .) |
| **mad maddie:** | **for my first pick? "because i'm awesome" by the dollyrots. or maybe "i hear noises" by tegan and sara . . . ?** |
| SnowAngel: | u do get multiple picks, ya know. we're gonna pass it around like all the other times we've done playlists. ready, set . . . go! |

Send    Cancel

Send    Cancel

## time out for . . .
# u and yr panis

| | |
|---|---|
| SnowAngel: | last one, best one. ready? |
| SnowAngel: | this one's from Benjamin Franklin: "The doors of wisdom are never shut . . ." |
| **mad maddie:** | **WITH MY PANIS!** |
| **mad maddie:** | **unless it's a revolving door, in which case it might be shut if my panis gets stuck in it. didn't my panis get stuck in a revolving door earlier on?** |
| zoegirl: | yes . . . but just think of all the great works that were born cuz of it!!!! |
| SnowAngel: | and now, darling bff's, it's time to let u loose with yr very own panises. |
| **mad maddie:** | **and quotes, don't forget the quotes** |
| SnowAngel: | if u don't have a squillion of 'em memorized— |
| **mad maddie:** | **and who does, other than zoe?** |
| zoegirl: | ha ha hahahaha |
| SnowAngel: | then go online, where u can find tons of great quotes, easy-peasy. AND MAY THE PANIS BE WITH U!!!!!! |

Send     Cancel

# what can u do 2 make
# the world a better place?

| | |
|---|---|
| SnowAngel: | oh, darlings!!!! our time together is—sniff, sniff—almost at an end! ☹ |
| **mad maddie:** | **ah, but angela. that's the thing about bff's . . . our time will NEVER come to an end.** |
| zoegirl: | not if we don't let it, anyway. |
| SnowAngel: | *wipes away tear and stands up staunchly* WHICH WE WILL NOT! |
| SnowAngel: | we get to choose, ya know? we get to choose what kind of friends to be—and no one can take that from us! |
| zoegirl: | also . . . not to insert too much deepness at the very end . . . but we also get to choose what kind of humans to be. which is kind of a huge deal, really. |
| **mad maddie:** | **i agree. this is our ONE LIFE, as far as we know, and if we don't make the most of it, then we kinda suck, don't we?** |
| SnowAngel: | well, to put it bluntly . . . yeah, i guess so. |
| zoegirl: | i don't want to suck. |
| SnowAngel: | i refuse to suck. |
| **mad maddie:** | **yeah? i'm a "spit, not swallow" gal myself, heh heh heh . . .** |
| SnowAngel: | 😖 |
| SnowAngel: | i thought we were being serious! |
| **mad maddie:** | **we can be serious and still make jokes, can't we?** |
| zoegirl: | but, um . . . yeah. let's get to the serious part. |
| zoegirl: | what r u gonna do to make the world a better place? |

| | |
|---|---|
| SnowAngel: | for reals? and no beauty pageant answers like "feed the starving orphans," not that that's a bad thing to do. |
| **mad maddie:** | **uh, feeding the starving orphans wld be a GREAT thing to do!** |
| **mad maddie:** | **but i think what angela means is . . . don't just spout off whatever sounds noble and grand.** |
| zoegirl: | yeah, cuz the thing is, U have something to offer the world that no one else does. |
| SnowAngel: | and so do yr bff's. *nods head rapidly* yup yup yup! |
| **mad maddie:** | **so . . . think about it. and don't run from it, don't be all, "ooo, this is stupid, who am \*i\* to change the world?"** |
| zoegirl: | we're not asking u to write a college essay, we swear. |
| SnowAngel: | just be real |
| zoegirl: | yeah. be real. |
| **mad maddie:** | **and change the world for the better . . . starting now, by committing to it on paper.** |
| SnowAngel: | in front of witnesses! ☺☺☺☺☺☺☺ |
| zoegirl: | u can do it! we believe in u!!!! |
| SnowAngel: | we luv u, bff's! |
| **mad maddie:** | **stay cool, stay kind, stay true! byeas for now . . .** |
| SnowAngel: | . . . but not forever!!!!!!!!! ♡ |

_____

_____

_____

_____

_____

_____

Send   Cancel

Send   Cancel

# bff

♡ ♡ ♡ ♡ ♡ ♡ ♡ ♡ ♡ ♡ ♡ ♡ ♡ ♡ ♡ ♡

Send      Cancel

♡ ♡ ♡ ♡ ♡ ♡ ♡ ♡ ♡ ♡ ♡ ♡ ♡ ♡ ♡ ♡

Send    Cancel

| | |
|---|---|
| SnowAngel: | *peeps head out from behind Great Cheese Puff in the sky* |
| SnowAngel: | peek-a-boo! |
| zoegirl: | hi, again! |
| **mad maddie:** | **faked ya out, didn't we? but c, that is our POWER and our MYSTERY. we will never leave, not really.** |
| SnowAngel: | we will always be here. |
| **mad maddie:** | **but not in a creepy stalker way.** |
| zoegirl: | just . . . oh, think of us as . . . the spirit of friendship. |
| SnowAngel: | with wings! fairy wings! I CLAIM PURPLE!!!!! |
| **mad maddie:** | **oh good god. i need nachos. can someone plz give me a big plate of nachos?** |
| SnowAngel: | yes, maddie. i will give u a big plate of nachos. *gives maddie big plate of nachos* |
| SnowAngel: | and all u bff's out there in neverland—don't worry, cuz i have something for y'all, too. |
| zoegirl: | wait . . . i thought *we* were the ones in neverland . . . ? |
| SnowAngel: | it all depends on how u look at it, now doesn't it? |
| **mad maddie:** | **so what do u have for them, a?** |
| SnowAngel: | actually, it's from all 3 of us. *brings zoe and maddie into a huddle and whispers excitedly* |
| zoegirl: | oh yeah! i remember! |
| **mad maddie:** | **riiiight, of course. duh!** |
| SnowAngel: | *grins* so go on. tell 'em. |
| **mad maddie:** | **well, just to warn u, there is a slight cheese factor to our parting gift. in fact, more than slight. but just deal with it.** |
| SnowAngel: | nothing wrong with cheese! |
| zoegirl: | our gift to u . . . |

♡ ♡ ♡ ♡ ♡ ♡ ♡ ♡ ♡ ♡ ♡ ♡ ♡ ♡ ♡

Send    Cancel

| | |
|---|---|
| **mad maddie:** | **. . . is U!** |
| SnowAngel: | pages and pages of U!!!!!! |
| zoegirl: | space for y'all to share your hopes and dreams . . . |
| **mad maddie:** | **or draw silly doodles . . .** |
| SnowAngel: | or paste in pics, or leave messages for each other, or WHATEVER! |
| zoegirl: | just have fun, that's all |
| **mad maddie:** | **and, hey. show it to us when ur done, will ya?** |
| SnowAngel: | *slings one arm around zoe and one arm around maddie* |
| SnowAngel: | we'll be here, sweeties. and we can't WAIT to see what u come up with. |

♡ ♡ ♡ ♡ ♡ ♡ ♡ ♡ ♡ ♡ ♡ ♡ ♡ ♡ ♡ ♡

Send    Cancel

♡ ♡ ♡ ♡ ♡ ♡ ♡ ♡ ♡ ♡ ♡ ♡ ♡ ♡ ♡ ♡

Send    Cancel

♡ ♡ ♡ ♡ ♡ ♡ ♡ ♡ ♡ ♡ ♡ ♡ ♡ ♡ ♡ ♡

Send    Cancel

# bff

○ ○ ○ ○ ○ ○ ○ ○ ○ ○ ○ ○ ○ ○ ○ ○

Send    Cancel

♡ ♡ ♡ ♡ ♡ ♡ ♡ ♡ ♡ ♡ ♡ ♡ ♡ ♡ ♡ ♡ ♡

**Send**    **Cancel**

# bff

$\heartsuit$ $\heartsuit$ $\heartsuit$ $\heartsuit$ $\heartsuit$ $\heartsuit$ $\heartsuit$ $\heartsuit$ $\heartsuit$ $\heartsuit$ $\heartsuit$ $\heartsuit$ $\heartsuit$ $\heartsuit$ $\heartsuit$ $\heartsuit$

[Send] [Cancel]

♡ ♡ ♡ ♡ ♡ ♡ ♡ ♡ ♡ ♡ ♡ ♡ ♡ ♡ ♡ ♡ ♡

Send     Cancel

_____

_____

_____

_____

_____

_____

_____

_____

_____

_____

_____

_____

_____

_____

_____

_____

_____

_____

_____

_____

_____

♡ ♡ ♡ ♡ ♡ ♡ ♡ ♡ ♡ ♡ ♡ ♡ ♡ ♡ ♡ ♡

248

Send    Cancel

♡ ♡ ♡ ♡ ♡ ♡ ♡ ♡ ♡ ♡ ♡ ♡ ♡ ♡ ♡ ♡

Send        Cancel

# bff

_____

_____

_____

_____

_____

_____

_____

_____

_____

_____

_____

_____

_____

_____

_____

_____

_____

_____

_____

_____

♡ ♡ ♡ ♡ ♡ ♡ ♡ ♡ ♡ ♡ ♡ ♡ ♡ ♡ ♡ ♡

250

**Send**     **Cancel**

**lauren myracle**

Send   Cancel

# About the Author

**Lauren Myracle** has written squillions of books for teens and tweens, including the *New York Times* bestselling *Internet Girls* books, *Bliss*, and *Rhymes with Witches*. Not until *bff*, however, has she giggled so wildly over such goofy best friend silliness. She hopes it makes you and your besties giggle, too!

Visit her on the web at laurenmyracle.com, will ya? Or else she will cry, and it is possible that a snot worm will creep from her nose. It has been known to happen.

The text in this book is set in 10-point Georgia, TheSans 9-Black, and ComicSans. This book was designed by Melissa Arnst and Interrobang Design Studio. The cell phone icons and many of the smiley faces were created by Celina Carvalho.